"I Want You, I've Been W

Control and good old-fashioned morals vaporized in the face of that declaration.

She wanted *him.* "Are you sure?"

"I've never been more certain of anything in my life."

She *thought* she was sure. But tomorrow how would she feel? Once she'd experienced lovemaking, would she still want him as much? What if that look of pure desire disappeared after she'd lost her virginity, only to be replaced by that icy protective shell she'd wrapped herself in the last time they'd woken up together?

Could he take that risk?

Could he *not?*

He ran his hands down her back, grazing the T-shirt— *his* shirt that she'd kept for *ten* years—until he reached…bare skin.

"I hope you know what you're doing, Miss Harrington."

Dear Reader,

Welcome to another fabulous month at Silhouette Desire, where we offer you the best in passionate, powerful and provocative love stories. You'll want to delve right in to our latest DYNASTIES: THE DANFORTHS title with Anne Marie Winston's highly dramatic *The Enemy's Daughter*—you'll never guess who the latest Danforth bachelor has gotten involved with! And the steam continues to rise when Annette Broadrick returns to the Desire line with a brand-new series, THE CRENSHAWS OF TEXAS. These four handsome brothers will leave you breathless, right from the first title, *Branded*.

Read a Silhouette Desire novel from *his* point of view in our new promotion MANTALK. Eileen Wilks continues this series with her highly innovative and intensely emotional story *Meeting at Midnight*. Kristi Gold continues her series THE ROYAL WAGER with another confirmed bachelor about to meet his match in *Unmasking the Maverick Prince*. How comfortable can *A Bed of Sand* be? Well, honey, if you're lying on it with the hero of Laura Wright's latest novel…who cares! And the always enjoyable Roxanne St. Claire, whom *Publishers Weekly* calls "an author who's on the fast track to making her name a household one," is scorching up the pages with *The Fire Still Burns*.

Happy reading,

Melissa Jeglinski

Melissa Jeglinski
Senior Editor, Silhouette Desire

Please address questions and book requests to:
Silhouette Reader Service
U.S.: 3010 Walden Ave., P.O. Box 1325, Buffalo, NY 14269
Canadian: P.O. Box 609, Fort Erie, Ont. L2A 5X3

The Fire Still Burns

ROXANNE ST. CLAIRE

Silhouette®

Desire

Published by Silhouette Books

America's Publisher of Contemporary Romance

SILHOUETTE BOOKS

ISBN 0-373-76608-4

THE FIRE STILL BURNS

Copyright © 2004 by Roxanne St. Claire

Visit Silhouette Books at www.eHarlequin.com

Printed in U.S.A.

ROXANNE ST. CLAIRE

began writing romance fiction in 1999 after nearly two decades as a public relations and marketing executive. Retiring from business to pursue a lifelong dream of writing romance is one of the most rewarding accomplishments in her life. The others are her happy marriage to a real-life hero and the daily joys of raising two young children. Roxanne writes mainstream romantic suspense, contemporary romance and women's fiction. Her work has received numerous awards, including the prestigious Heart to Heart Award, the Golden Opportunity Award and the Gateway Award. An active member of the Romance Writers of America, Roxanne lives in Florida and currently writes—and raises children—full-time. She loves to hear from readers through e-mail at roxannestc@aol.com and snail mail at P. O. Box 372909, Satellite Beach, FL 32937. Visit her Web site at www.roxannestclaire.com.

For Stephanie Maurer, who invited me to play in her sandbox and then made it so much fun I never want to leave! Thank you for the perfect editorial touch.

And for Lizzie B and Sally Jo,
who introduced me to the endless summers of Newport, Rhode Island, and offered a lifetime of friendship, as well. You'll recognize the carriage house, girls.

One

The charred remains of Edgewater stood like a massive black-and-silver mountain in the middle of a field of fried brown grass. Colin McGrath gazed at the rubble of what was once one of Newport's most glorious summer mansions.

Edgewater was gone. And with it, a piece of Newport's great "Gilded Age." The architect in him mourned the loss of any magnificent structure, since he believed that they all had a soul of their own. But the purist in him wanted to thrust his fist in the air and holler, "Yes!" Good riddance to overopulent, out-of-proportion, Italianate mausoleums. There were still enough of them in Newport, Rhode Island, to attract tourists by the thousands.

In his opinion, excessive extravagance had gone out with the old millennium. In the case of Edgewater, the exit had been accelerated by one strategically placed lightning strike, and then helped along by high winds and a year-long drought. Mother Nature's cleanup campaign. And what had started as a favor to someone dear to him had become a personal mission.

Colin's vision for Edgewater's replacement was so vivid, he really didn't need the sketches in the worn portfolio tucked under his arm.

Just the thought brought a smile to his face as he sauntered toward the three-story carriage house, the only structure on the historic property that had survived the fire.

The finest architects in the country had been called to compete for this job. Colin paused and rolled his head a bit, working out a crick in his neck. He glanced at the sea of dark Brooks Brothers-type suits and stiff white shirts gathered in groups along the wraparound patio. A few women wore the female version of the same uniform.

Not a ponytail, earring or a pair of jeans in the whole gang. Until now.

He took the front steps two at a time, aware that conversations stopped and heads turned at his arrival. Nothing new. He'd been ruffling the feathers of the architecture world since he'd descended upon it six years ago. One thing was for sure: everyone in this group knew his name and his reputation.

But he hadn't bothered to research the other firms. The only real competition for this job was Hazelwood and Harrington, and somewhere in this bunch was some muck-a-muck from that 150-year-old institution. Maybe even Eugene Harrington himself. It didn't matter who H&H had sent to compete— there was only one person on their payroll he cared about and they certainly wouldn't have sent *her*. No doubt His Highness Harrington kept the princess locked in an ivory tower. Protecting her from wolves…especially ones with long hair.

"The presentations have already started," a gray-haired undertaker type said to him, making little effort to hide the "you're late" disdain in his voice. "You need to check in with the secretary in the house."

Colin nodded his thanks, unfazed by the warning. Adrian Gilmore, the current owner of Edgewater, would meet with his ten candidates alphabetically. Colin might not know the competition, but he'd made sure he knew everything about the eccentric British billionaire looking to reconstruct his burned castle on Bellevue Avenue. Colin fully intended to land the job.

Only he had absolutely no intention of rebuilding Edgewater.

A young woman holding a clipboard stood in the two-story entryway, pacing in front of a set of closed double doors. Behind them, in what he assumed was the solarium, Gilmore was undoubtedly holding court—er, conducting presentations.

"You must be Mr. McGrath," she said, slowing her step to let her gaze meander over his casual dress, lingering for a moment on the tiny gold hoop in his right ear.

He gave her a self-deprecating smile. "How'd you guess?"

"You're the only person on my list who hasn't checked in yet." Her eyes sparkled with a flirtatious gleam. "And the only man not wearing a tie."

He winked and lowered his voice to a conspiratorial tone. "I don't want to choke."

She laughed lightly in response.

"Tell me he hasn't reached *M*…yet." He glanced at the closed doors.

"You just made it," she said, chastising him with a wave of her pen. "You're up next, right after Miss Harrington."

"*Miss* Harrington?" For a split second, the world tilted on its axis. "Grace Harrington?"

Before the woman could answer, the double doors opened, pouring light into the dim entryway. Framed by the doorway and backlit by golden rays of sunshine, the woman who'd haunted his dreams for ten years stood looking as though she'd been beamed down from heaven.

Gracie.

For a moment, he didn't breathe.

She smoothed a lock of pale blond hair, as if by some remote chance a single strand might have defied the rules of nature and wandered out of place. Her hair was shorter than he remembered, grazing her shoulders like blunt-cut satin. But her face hadn't changed in ten years. Unless he called getting more beautiful a change.

She still had a milky-smooth complexion, eyes the color of spring moss and cheekbones designed by an artist. When she smiled at the receptionist, the dimples he remembered so well deepened, zinging arrows straight into his heart.

The memory of Grace Harrington could make his blood hot and his body hard. The sight of her nearly did him in.

"Hey, Gracie," he said quietly, purposely staying out of the light.

Her eyes flashed, and for one second—no, for one millionth of a nanosecond—he saw them register with shock and...pleasure. The flicker dulled immediately into a blank stare.

"Excuse me?"

Which translated loosely into "no one on earth calls me Gracie and lives."

He stepped out of the shadows. "Colin McGrath." He held out his hand as though...as though they'd never had an intimate moment. Of course, that would depend on the definition of *intimate*.

She responded with a blank stare.

"Carnegie Mellon? Your freshman year?" He drank in her pretty face, lingering for a second on her slender throat and the exposed skin peeking from her ivory suit. He swore he could remember exactly what that skin tasted like. He leaned forward and added in a quiet voice, "The *Buggy* Races?"

A warm flush darkened her cheeks. She obviously remembered the night *Lady* Harrington had been anything but *lady*like.

"Colin. Of course." Her smooth New England tones remained rich with upper-class elegance. "I'd heard you'd opened your own firm, in, uh, Pittsburgh." Was that a note of condescension when she mentioned his humble hometown?

But at least she knew something about him. Had she done an Internet search and followed his career as he'd followed hers? His occasional visits to various search engines had revealed that she'd obtained her Masters at the Rhode Island School of Design and joined her father's revered architectural firm. He knew she lived in Boston and, son of a gun, somehow he'd managed to find out that she hadn't gotten married yet.

"I'm still in Pittsburgh," he said. "But I get around."

Her eyes darted to his earring and his open collar. "I'm sure you do."

Ouch.

"Nice to see nothing's changed," he said dryly.

Nothing *had* changed. Gracie was still a goddess who loathed him for the one night she'd fallen off her pedestal right into the arms—and the bed—of an unworthy rogue.

"Nothing's changed?" She raised one delicate brow in question and shifted her portfolio from one hand to the other.

He took a step nearer to her, catching a whiff of lavender and stealing some of her personal space. "You're still…" he grinned as her eyes widened "…gorgeous."

"Mr. McGrath." The receptionist's voice pulled him out of the depths of Gracie's eyes. "Mr. Gilmore is ready for you now."

He saw Gracie's narrow shoulders relax in pure relief. "Good luck with your presentation."

He nodded a casual thanks, but managed to block her exit with a step toward the solarium doors. "Let's have lunch when I'm finished."

That spark lit her eyes again but it died quickly, replaced by a cool, tight smile. "Thank you, but I have to drive back to Boston this afternoon."

Of course she'd say no. For the four years they were both at Carnegie Mellon, she'd barely been able to hide her utter contempt when their paths crossed on campus or in the architecture department. She would look away, without the slightest acknowledgement. And he knew damn well she'd juggled her course schedule to avoid having him as a grad student teaching assistant.

But ten years had passed. Nearly a third of his life, and hers. Someone or something had put them in the same place at the same time. Gram McGrath would call it his inexplicable good luck. "The moment you arrived the devil was having a fight with his wife, Colin McGrath," she'd say, using her expression for the unusual combination of rain and sunshine. "So you were born under a rainbow and showered with good luck." And Gram would twist his ear as though he were still five years old if she found out he'd run into this rainfall of luck and hadn't stopped to get really good and wet.

"Come on, Gracie. Tell Daddy you stayed to check out the competition."

The secretary cleared her throat.

Gracie's *faux* smile wavered, and he saw a tiny vein pulse in her throat. He'd kissed that vein.

"We're not worried about competition," she said as she managed to step around him. "Hazelwood and Harrington built Edgewater in the nineteenth century and we'll rebuild it in the twenty-first."

"Mr. McGrath, Mr. Gilmore is waiting."

The humor had left the secretary's voice, replaced by an edge of irritation.

"Goodbye, Colin. It was nice to see you."

He wouldn't let Gracie go without a fight. He'd done that once before. "No." He reached for her arm and she snatched it away as if she'd been burned. *Easy, boy.* "We should talk. About this project."

"What's the holdup, McGrath?" Adrian Gilmore's British accent echoed from the solarium.

Colin pinned Gracie with narrowed eyes, and took a

chance. "I need to tell you something," he said slowly, deliberately. "About the night…of the Buggy Races."

Her skin paled and she raised a defiant chin. "Ancient history, I assure you."

"Diane!" Colin heard the scrape of Gilmore's chair against hardwood. "Just skip McGrath and go straight to Perkins."

Damn it. He touched her shoulder, lightly this time. "Wait for me, Gracie."

Before she had a chance to respond, he strode into the solarium and across the expanse toward Adrian Gilmore's desk. "Don't even think about skipping this, Adrian. I've got the winning designs right here."

The Burger Boy billionaire didn't laugh. "I like confidence, McGrath, but don't test my patience again."

"The only thing I plan to test is your imagination, Adrian." Colin shook hands with the youthful-looking fast-food tycoon and gave him a cocky smile that belied the war going on in his head.

He opened his portfolio, took out his first sketch, and tried to concentrate.

Would she stay? And if she did, should he tell her the truth? That during the one night they'd shared all he'd done was watch her sleep it off?

She had awakened in his bed and in his arms, hungover for the first—and he was willing to bet—the last time in her life, believing that he'd taken her virginity. But she wouldn't listen to his denials. He couldn't really blame her for being so certain about what had happened. Not when they'd awakened with her in a state of total undress and his bed in a classic morning-after mess. Would she believe him, now? Or was ten years too late and too long ago?

"What the hell is *that?*" Gilmore asked, pointing to the black-and-white elevation draft that Colin had pulled out.

"That, Adrian, is Pineapple House, and it stood on this

property a hundred and fifty years before Edgewater. I'm going to design and build it for you."

Just as he began his pitch, Colin realized that should he succeed, it would probably cost him any chance with Gracie he'd ever have.

But Adrian suddenly looked very interested.

Grace darted from the carriage house, ignoring curious glances from the other architects. She slowed her step as she reached her Audi, parked in front of Edgewater's massive Bellevue Avenue entrance. She'd snagged a shady spot, having arrived, of course, an hour early for her "date with destiny"—as her roommate had called the important meeting over breakfast that morning.

Allie had no idea how right she'd been. But not because of the magnitude of the new business pitch Grace had just made. Instead, destiny had appeared in the form of a decade-old memory that never failed to rock her foundation.

Colin McGrath. Looking bad to the bone and good enough to eat.

She pulled her keychain out of her portfolio and fumbled with the unlock button. She had to get out of here before he finished his presentation. Adrian Gilmore was giving each architect fifteen minutes and not one second more.

Opening the door, she took a deep breath and one last look at the remains of Edgewater.

But instead of nature's destruction, she saw…milk-chocolate eyes with flecks of gold and silky black hair just begging to be released from a simple leather tie and fingercombed.

Oh, brother.

What had happened to the powerful, confident, visionary architect who'd just met with Adrian Gilmore? Colin McGrath had happened. One seductive smile, one whispered invitation, and he'd flat-out demolished her professional high. It wasn't the first time she'd crumbled from the sheer force of that man. But damn, it would be the last.

Wait for me, Gracie.

Why did his purposely mocking nickname still send an electrical jolt to every cell in her body? Because it rolled off his tongue in the most irreverent, playful…and *provocative* way?

She exhaled slowly and studied the oak-lined avenue that had once bustled with society ladies and clattering buggies.

Buggies? What made her think of those?

I need to tell you something…about the night of the Buggy Races.

Her heart kicked up a beat as her head reeled with possibilities.

Maybe he wanted to apologize. Which was ridiculous because he'd done what any red-blooded twenty-year-old man would do when a plastered freshman who'd been following him for seven months threw herself at him.

Maybe he wanted to ingratiate himself with her—and her father—somehow. Maybe his business was failing and he needed work. Which was ridiculous because she'd heard he was outstandingly successful.

Maybe he wanted to…repeat history. Now that was the most ridiculous scenario of all because…because…

She placed her portfolio in the back seat of her car, and then opened the driver's door. *Finish the thought, Grace.*

Because she was not interested in a troublemaker like Colin McGrath. Period.

He was brash, bold and dangerous. She'd found that out the hard way ten years ago.

But what could he want to tell her?

Squaring her shoulders, she slammed the car door without getting in and started across the drive, past the charred stump of a two-hundred-year-old elm that had sustained a lightning strike.

She really didn't want to leave without having seen the water. And he probably wouldn't even notice if she stood by the cliffs for a few moments.

Yeah, right.

Her heels scraped along the crispy grass as she rounded what was left of the north wing of the thirty-thousand square foot "summer cottage." Two months since the fire and, amazingly, the bitter smells of soot and ash still mixed with the briny scent that wafted up from the ocean.

Ahead of her lay the icy waters of Rhode Island Sound, with only a waist-high barrier of marble balustrades to prevent any of the more irrational residents of Edgewater from flinging themselves over the famed cliffs of Newport.

And talk about *irrational*...why hadn't she gotten into her car and disappeared before he came out?

"Oh, God." Her quiet moan hung in the dry northerly breeze that always arrived in Newport just as the tourists left. She stared at the curls of whitecaps against the blue-black sea and gripped the railing.

Everybody made juvenile mistakes in college, didn't they? Everybody got drunk once and did something foolish in frat houses. *Didn't they?*

Well, maybe *they* did. But Grace Harrington didn't. No matter how killer a crush she had on the cutest guy on campus. No matter how many inhibitions were destroyed by Southern Comfort. No matter how many excuses she invented. She'd ended up in the one place she should have avoided. His bed.

"Thanks for waiting."

She started at the sound of his voice, turning toward it and sucking in a silent breath. He sauntered across the charred lawn, the scorched remains of Edgewater as his breathtaking backdrop. Satan himself emerging from hell to stir up trouble and break some hearts.

"I really hoped you'd stay." His admission came with a soft laugh and a tilt of his head that caused sunlight to glint off his gold earring. Who would have thought that one little bit of jewelry could be so…sexy?

She backed up into the marble railing, a mental image of the whitecaps forty feet below flashing in her mind. But what was more dangerous? The sea behind her, or the devil in front? "You weren't in there very long," she said.

He continued his approach. "I didn't need much time."

She tried to hold his gaze, but couldn't resist a quick inspection of his still-impressive physique. She had to look up at him, even though in heels she was easily five-seven; he topped six feet by two inches. Over the years, his chest, always substantial from an array of sports, had expanded to a broad, powerful plane and through his loose linen shirt she could see the outline of solid, muscular arms. A pair of worn blue jeans fit snug over narrow hips. *Jeans.* To meet with one of the richest men in the world.

Only Colin McGrath, the rebel without a care.

"But you weren't in there for five minutes," she insisted.

He shrugged and took another step closer, giving her the opportunity to study his face, which was, unfortunately, as appealing as his body. His features had matured into more masculine, handsome lines, all traces of boyishness gone, leaving hollowed cheeks and a square jaw in their place. The deliberate shadow of a beard suited a man who pitched a multi-million dollar account in denim. Shaving was no doubt optional. His bedroom-brown eyes were still fringed with sinfully long lashes.

"I had an incentive to get out of there fast." He lifted his lips into a mocking half smile. "Besides, it only took a few minutes to nail the deal."

"To nail the—" She narrowed her eyes. "You're lying." Even as she made the accusation, she knew it couldn't be true.

Colin McGrath's honesty was as much a part of him as the signature ponytail that bound his shoulder-length hair.

"He liked my ideas." With a grin, his gaze drifted down her face…and lower. The smile slowly disappeared as he returned to her eyes. "You look good, Gracie."

Her stomach fluttered. She crossed her arms and leaned against the railing, something she ordinarily wouldn't do in a white silk suit. But her legs suddenly felt woefully inadequate at their job.

"Did he tell you that? That he liked your ideas?" Adrian had said the same thing to *her* before she'd left the solarium.

"He didn't have to."

Damn his confidence. He'd always oozed it. Confidence and candor. That's what made Colin McGrath tick. "He's only halfway through the presentations," she reminded him.

"True enough," he agreed. "And the competition is fierce. No doubt H&H is putting a mountain of resources into this one."

Had she detected a tinge of envy in his voice? It couldn't be. He'd had a chance to work for the biggest and best, but he'd turned her father down. Refused to do a second interview, rumor had it.

"We don't have any special inside track, if that's what you're implying."

He smiled and dipped his head. "I didn't mean that, Gracie."

He didn't have to. The whole architecture world was watching how H&H handled this bid, and the whole company was watching how she handled herself to get the business.

Edgewater had become the Holy Grail of architecture and she wanted it. If only to prove to her colleagues, and the rest of the industry, once and for all, that she wasn't just the boss's daughter. She was a talented architect in her own right. It wouldn't hurt to get her father to notice that, too.

She clenched her jaw and raised her chin. "H&H has the expertise, the talent, the staff and the history that no other firm can offer. We don't need to pull strings to get this business. We are the best firm to rebuild Edgewater."

He chuckled softly and tipped her chin back down with a tap of a single finger. "Save your sales pitch for Gilmore, Gracie. I don't intend to rebuild Edgewater."

He *didn't?* "Then what are you doing here? All of the firms are pitching a rebuild of the burned mansion."

"Let them." He shrugged and turned toward the mountain of ash behind him. "I don't want to rebuild any mansions."

This *was* intriguing. So were the few dark hairs that escaped his open collar. "Then what did you just propose to Adrian?"

He hooked his thumbs on his belt loops and gave her a long, intense look. "I'll tell you over lunch."

"I don't think so."

"Wouldn't the board of H&H like to know what the competition is up to?" He leaned closer. He smelled like soap and woods and…autumn. "Information like that could affect the entire spec creative design. You could be the company hero, Gracie."

God, he was good. "That's blackmail, McGrath."

"Nah," he shook his head. "It's lunch. If I were going to blackmail you, Gracie, I'd go for something stronger."

Like Southern Comfort. She pointedly gazed over his shoulder to study the graceful roofline of the carriage house and the centuries-old trees on its lawn, and then inched to the right.

"Thank you, but I really need to get going. I want to start the design work." She shot him a warning look. "We still might get this business, regardless of your self-confidence and misplaced beliefs."

"The only one who has misplaced beliefs is you." He mirrored her sidestep and held her in place with a razor-sharp gaze. "I told you, Gracie, I want to talk to you about something personal."

She didn't want to hear what he had to say. *Gee, Gracie, I don't think I ever told you that you were great on the dining room floor, on the stairs, in my room.*

He reached for her hand and wrapped his fingers confidently around hers. "Come on, Gracie. It's just lunch."

Damn it all. She'd sworn she'd never go anywhere near Colin McGrath again. She'd sworn she'd never take a drink of anything stronger than green tea. And she'd sworn she'd never give her body to another man until she was completely and totally in love.

She'd kept all three promises. Until today.

"All right."

Two

For once Colin was glad he'd left his Harley at home. He'd made the long drive to Newport in his only slightly more client-friendly German sports car.

Not that he wouldn't like to see Gracie hike that body-hugging skirt up those mile-high thighs and climb on the back of his hog. But that would really be pushing his luck. And right now, his luck was holding just fine.

"Let's go down to the harbor," he suggested as he opened the Boxster's passenger door. "You'll like Zelda's."

As she got into his low-slung car, Gracie's skirt rode up enough to offer a tantalizing glimpse of those same heavenly thighs. He couldn't resist a teasing wink when she looked up and caught him staring.

"I do like Zelda's," she assured him, tugging at the hem before she reached for the seat belt. "I went to grad school in Providence and spent a lot of time in Newport."

He got the messages—all of them. She knew her way

around, she had a legitimate degree, and don't ogle the merchandise.

Sliding behind the wheel, he reached in front of her to move his portfolio. "Sorry, no back seat. I can put this in the trunk."

"I'll hold it." She placed the leather case on her lap, effectively hiding his view of her legs.

"Wanna see my etchings?" he asked, his voice rich with teasing seduction as he tapped on the case. "Go ahead. You can take a look."

She gave him a wide-eyed look of surprise. "You'd share your ideas with the competition?"

With a shrug, he stabbed the key in the ignition. "Hazelwood and Harrington would never consider these competitive ideas. I have a whole different vision for Edgewater."

Her fingers toyed with the zipper, then she folded her hands together. "I'm not interested."

"Sure you are." Pulling into Bellevue traffic, he turned toward town. "I'm not worried that you're going to run back to Boston and copy them."

"I would never dream of stealing your ideas."

He spared her a quick glance and shifted gears. "Of course not. I'm certain you have plenty of your own."

As she crossed her arms, he could practically feel her bristle next to him. "That I do."

"RISD's a great school." He knew the prestigious Rhode Island School of Design well enough to use the common "Rizdee" abbreviation. "I have other friends who went to grad school there, too."

If she took note of the fact that he knew where she went to graduate school, she didn't let it show. "I loved it. Providence is a terrific town."

"As terrific as Pittsburgh?"

That earned him a sharp look. Too many memories?

"Carnegie Mellon is also an excellent school for architecture," she responded. "You must like the city to have stayed there."

Was that an indictment he heard in her voice? It had to be. And wasn't that at the heart of her pained expression every time the conversation danced near the topic of what they'd done…or hadn't?

He was from a construction family—a broken one, at that—in the Steel City, and she'd been born, raised and coddled among New England's finest bloodlines. The kind with ancestors who arrived on the *Mayflower,* not in steerage on their way to Ellis Island.

"I have a good client base and a lot of friends in Pittsburgh," he said, shifting his tone into neutral and the car into third as they rounded a curve and caught the breathtaking vista of the Atlantic Ocean. "My dad lives there and my two brothers come back a lot to visit."

"Where do they live?"

"Cameron's in New York, working on Wall Street, and Quinn just bagged his real estate development job in Manhattan and moved to an island in Florida." He tapped the brake as traffic slowed near town.

"Really? Why did he do that?"

"He's in *looove.*" Colin rolled his eyes, thinking of Quinn's insane engagement, announced on a billboard. "Love makes you do crazy things."

"So I've heard."

At her dry tone, he glanced at her again. "No firsthand experience with that, Gracie?"

For a moment, she didn't say anything, but pierced him with a meaningful look. "With crazy, yes, but not love."

The arrow hit its mark. Without thinking, he took his hand off the gear shift and placed it on top of her folded ones. How could he say this? *It wasn't crazy? All you did was pass out?*

A horn honked behind him and he had to turn his attention back to the road.

Over lunch. He'd tell her over lunch.

No more double entendres, Grace Harrington. Don't flirt with him. Don't get comfortable with him.

Grace's head rang with warning bells. She took a deep breath, a move that caused her shoulder to brush his powerful arm. They had even more electrical body contact every time he took a turn at just a hair over the speed limit. He was warm and solid and…enticing.

She'd made a mistake once before with this man. Never again.

She should have leaped from the car when he parked across from the restaurant on Thames Street. Instead, she waited as he came around and opened her door.

As she climbed out of the car, she glanced at the flapping green awning bearing the name Zelda's in funky, hot-pink lettering. She'd had a few dates here when she was in grad school. In every case, the food far exceeded the company.

This time, she doubted she'd even be able to eat. Colin Mc-Grath had managed to tie her stomach up in knots. And lower than her stomach, too. But he'd had that effect on her the first time she'd seen him, just days after she arrived at Carnegie Mellon as a freshman.

She'd spotted him in the architecture library, a tall, lanky, good-looking upper-classman whom she quickly learned had a reputation as a heartbreaker. But her crush had started the day he smiled at her…and ended the morning she woke up in a warm, rumpled bed on the third floor of the Sigma Nu house, wearing nothing but a CMU T-shirt, size extra large.

The memory of his hot, hard body, fully aroused and neatly pressed against her backside as she curled into him, almost took her breath away.

This was the same man.

She couldn't forget that.

"Know why the roof is slanted like that?" He pointed to the unusual angle above three stories of brick and brownstone.

"To collect water and bring it to the cistern for the brewery," she responded. "At least that was its purpose a hundred years ago."

He laughed and took her hand as they started across the street. "Guess I'm not going to impress you with little-known structural facts." He weaved his fingers between hers, sending sparks up her arm and more flutters to her stomach.

Did he really want to impress her? This was business. *Business.* And they were *competitors.*

When he opened the polished wood door of Zelda's, she took the opportunity to release her hand from his, inhaling the smoky aroma of steak and onions instead of the musky scent that clung to him.

"Oh, I left my portfolio and handbag in my car." She patted her suit jacket pockets, feeling only her phone and keys. "I don't have my wallet."

"Unless you're going to show me pictures of your kids, Gracie, you don't need your wallet. It's my treat." He put his hand on her back and guided her toward the hostess. Then suddenly, his lips were against her ear, his breath vibrating the tiny hairs on the back of her neck. "No kids yet, right, Gracie?"

"Welcome to Café Zelda." A surfer-blond hostess locked her wide-eyed gaze on Colin, all but batting her eyelashes at him. "Table for two?"

To his credit, he didn't flirt back, but kept his hand firmly on Grace's lower back. As they zigzagged through a maze of white-linen-clad tables, she kept her attention on walls festooned with photos of America's Cup crews, chanting a silent mantra. *This is a business lunch. A business lunch.*

Nothing more. Nothing less. It was perfectly appropriate

for him to place a casual hand on her back. Perfectly appropriate to exchange some personal information. Perfectly appropriate and yet, *intimate.*

Just like the undersized table for two they were given next to a window. Once seated, after they'd accepted menus and listened to the specials, she decided to get the personal stuff out of the way as fast as possible. Then they could concentrate on business.

"No children," she told him without preamble. His online biography made no mention of a wife or children, but sometimes they didn't. Her heart knocked a little, but she gave him a direct look and asked, "How about you?"

He responded with that devilish smile again, slow and easy and bone-melting. "Well, I have a six-year-old business. Does that count? It's certainly as demanding of my time as any child."

Out of habit, she straightened the silverware, lining up the knife and fork with exact precision. "Your firm is McGrath, Inc., right?" Knowing that much didn't reveal that she'd followed his professional progress.

"Yes. And like most six-year-olds, it's small, but mighty." He leaned casually on the table, seemingly in no hurry to pick up a menu. The afternoon light trickled through wood blinds, highlighting the hint of stubble on his cheeks, giving his face an achingly handsome shadow.

"So things are going well?" she asked, turning her attention to a coffee cup to set the handle at a neat ninety-degree angle.

When she looked up, he was grinning at her. "You might say that."

Of course, she'd read about his avant-garde designs and the many awards he'd won for unconventional and eclectic structures. The opera house in Oregon had been featured in *Newsweek.* "You have quite a reputation for…the unusual."

"I like to break rules." He laughed softly, putting his hand on hers. "And either you're nervous as hell or compulsively neat."

Both. "I like order." She tucked her hands on her lap and gave him a challenging look. "Are you planning to break rules with the rebuild of Edgewater?"

"I have no plans to rebuild Edgewater, Gracie. I told you that."

A trickle of concern meandered down her spine. What was he up to, and could it mean H&H might not get the business? Regardless of his dreamy eyes and blinding smile, she had to remember that this man was her competition for the one assignment she wanted—no, needed—to establish herself in the industry. And emerge from the cocoon her father had put her in years ago.

"Then what did you propose to Gilmore?" she asked casually.

He raised an eyebrow. "I thought you were worried about professional impropriety."

"You don't have to give away trade secrets, Colin. Just the general idea."

"Fair enough." He picked up a menu and handed it to her. "Let's order first and then I'll tell you." He paused, the light of humor gone from his eyes. "Over dessert, I have something else to tell you."

Gracie swallowed and leaned forward. This had to end. With as much class and cool as she could muster, she had to end this torture. "Colin, listen to me."

His captivated expression told her he was doing just that.

"Everyone is entitled to their mistakes in life and they pay for them in their own way." She felt the heat burn her cheeks, but forced herself to continue. "Would you be kind enough to avoid the subject of...of our brief encounter in college?"

He opened his mouth to say something, but she held up her hand, her heart crashing like a wrecking ball against her chest. "In case you are of a mind to relive the past, please understand. I don't want to make excuses for my behavior. I just fell under the wrong influence one night, that's all. Please. Don't mention it again."

She could have sworn his eyes darkened. Well, what did he expect? Did he think she wanted to rehash her ignoble loss of virginity? Did he want her to admit she didn't remember anything, not a single moment of an event that most girls can at least turn into a decent diary entry?

"You're safe for the rest of this meal," he said, his voice as smooth and cool as black satin. "But I can't make any promises about the future."

Gracie opened the menu. "There won't be any future," she said with certainty.

Brief encounter?
The wrong influence?

How could he have forgotten how much she reviled him? She wasn't bothered about losing her virginity, drunk in a frat house. She was really pained about losing her virginity *with him,* a blue-collar bad boy from Pittsburgh.

One whose success was so questionable that she worried about paying for her own lunch. No reason to dissuade her of that notion. Money didn't mean anything to him. Especially now that he had it.

"So tell me about your plans for Edgewater," she said after the waiter left. She kept her hands daintily clasped on the edge of the table, apparently finished reorganizing Zelda's place settings. Her lovely face looked composed, her lips tilted in a gracious smile.

Cool, calm and in control, as always. She'd taken care of her uncomfortable business and now she could be elegant Grace Harrington again.

He reached across the small table and unclasped her hands, lacing his fingers through hers. "Don't be so sure of everything, Gracie."

The color drained from her cheeks and she tugged against his hand. "What are you talking about?"

"There might very well be a *future*. Who knows? There are lots of jobs that use two firms." His fingers lightly stroked the creamy skin of her hand. "We may get the opportunity to work together someday."

"I doubt that."

"Why?" He released his hold. "You think H&H wouldn't get its hands dirty with a little boutique firm in Pittsburgh?"

Her eyes narrowed at him. "I didn't say that." She smoothed her napkin on her lap. "As a matter of fact, you're the one who wouldn't even interview with H&H after you got out of grad school."

She *knew* that? How much did she know about his one conversation with Eugene Harrington?

"I never wanted to work for a large firm, Gracie," he explained as he lifted his water glass. "I have nothing against Hazelwood and Harrington. Your father—and his father and I believe his father, too—all have exquisite architectural designs to their credit."

"And *his* father," she added. "Who designed Edgewater."

He took a sip and considered how best to respond to that. "I understand you have deep familial ties to the old building, Gracie, but don't be too disappointed when Adrian Gilmore opts for a different structure."

"What do you mean?"

"Pineapple House," he said simply.

"Pineapple—the old house that stood on the property before Edgewater?"

For some reason, it pleased and relieved him that she knew the history before the mansion. "Yes, Pineapple House. It was built in 1743, the Golden Age—not to be confused with the 'Gilded Age'—of Newport."

She gave him a confused look. "What does Pineapple House have to do with Edgewater today?"

"I proposed that Adrian let me design and reconstruct a replica of Pineapple House instead of Edgewater. I suggested he go a hundred and fifty years further back in history and build a tribute to the sea captains who inhabited and grew Newport from a settlement to a city. The men who brought pineapples back from the West Indies and started the tradition of equating that fruit with a warm welcome."

"I know the symbolism and history," she assured him. "But the original Pineapple House was torn down to build Edgewater. There's no reliable record of what it looked like— you'd just be creating a brand new house. Adrian wants to preserve history."

"I will preserve history." He leaned forward, lowering his voice to a whisper. "I have two-hundred-and-fifty-year-old documents that describe the original structure."

Her eyes became mint-green circles. "What? How? Where?"

There was a limit to how much he'd share, and he drew the line at his secret weapon. Plus, if she knew why Pineapple House was so important to him, he'd lose the distinct advantage he gained with the impersonal motivation of "business." "I can't reveal my sources."

She gave him a skeptical look. "Do you have sketches?"

"Detailed."

For a moment, she turned to the window, lost in thought. Then she snagged his gaze again. "A wooden two-story dwelling, no matter how authentic and enchanting it is, will not be grand enough for Gilmore."

"I'll agree that Pineapple House isn't opulent. On the contrary. But it was first, Gracie. That building stood a hundred years before some New York banker named Andrew Smith leveled it and erected a monument to his greed."

"Andrew Smith was the first client of H&H," she responded. "My great-great-grandfather started an architectural dynasty with the profits from the design of Edgewater. It may have been a monument to Andrew Smith's success, but it was also the foundation on which my whole family's business was built."

He knew this would be at the core of the H&H pitch for the business. He sensed that it wouldn't carry a lot of weight with Gilmore, either. "Pineapple House epitomizes the true history of Newport—"

"So does Edgewater!" she shot back.

"Edgewater represents the time when money ran amuck, Gracie, when monstrosities of marble and gold were constructed for the sole purpose of hosting one over-the-top party a year."

She regarded him with narrowed eyes for a long moment. "Why are you so passionate about this?"

As usual, he wasn't doing a bang-up job of keeping this *impersonal.* "I'm passionate about everything."

She gave him a wary look. "What do you care about the history of Newport?"

"I care about heritage as much as history," he said, purposely vague.

"Then surely you understand my family's heritage is tied up with Edgewater."

He nodded in assent. "I believe it's crucial to incorporate history *and* heritage into any structure I design. Newport's been around since the 1600s. There are plenty of nineteenth-century mansions on Bellevue Avenue, Gracie. I'd like to see Adrian Gilmore…" he gave her a cocky smile "…break the rules."

She dabbed at the condensation around her water glass with a napkin. "Actually, it's an interesting idea, Colin, I'll admit it." She folded the napkin, dry side out, and put it back on her lap. "But don't be fooled by Adrian's laissez-faire attitude bought by fast-food billions. He desperately wants to be accepted in the upper echelons of society. Edgewater represents that more than anything."

She was right about Adrian's desire, but not about Edge-water representing guaranteed acceptance into society. "I think you're wrong."

Her look was pure challenge. "I think I'm right."

At that moment, his cell phone beeped a quiet melody. Gracie reached in her jacket pocket.

"No, it's mine," he said, unclipping the tiny gadget from his belt to check the ID. Caller unknown.

"Mine is vibrating." She pulled out a similar device from her pocket with an apologetic laugh. "Lunch in the new millennium. Do you mind?"

"Go ahead," he nodded, pressing the Talk button on his.

As soon as he said hello, he recognized Adrian Gilmore's distinctive East London clipped tones. "McGrath, I like your ideas. You might just have something with this Pineapple House."

Gracie suddenly turned to her side, a frown creasing her brow. Poor thing. Didn't make the cut. Hey, for all he knew, there might be no cut. Just Pineapple House.

"Glad to hear it," Colin said to Adrian. "When do we start?"

"Not so fast, mate. I think you need a bit more time to work on the designs."

He didn't respond, trying to hear what Gracie was whispering into her phone.

"How can we possibly do that?" she asked her caller.

"What did you have in mind?" Colin asked.

"Three weeks in Newport, McGrath, on me. Think of it as a working vacation."

"Vacation?"

"Vacation?" He looked up at Gracie's eerie echo of his word.

"I think you're dead on about getting a feel for the history of the property," Adrian continued. "I'd like you to move into the carriage house immediately and live there for three weeks. I think that's enough time to soak up the atmosphere and history and come up with a great design."

Gracie lined up her silverware—*again*—and listened intently into her phone. "Three weeks?" she asked.

Who was she talking to?

"Three weeks?" he repeated into his own phone. "And then I have the job?"

"Well, not exactly," Adrian responded with a quick laugh. "I've narrowed my choice down to two firms who have presented diametrically different ideas—both brilliant, but wholly opposing concepts. I'm asking both of you to spend the same time on the Edgewater property before you submit final designs."

Gracie nodded and said something he didn't catch. But a spine-tingling sense of anticipation started to seep through him. The familiar warmth of good luck.

"Then you'll make a decision in six weeks?" Colin asked.

"No. Three. You'll both be staying at the carriage house at the same time, participating in the same exercise."

Was Gilmore really saying what he *thought* he was saying? "At the same time?"

"That's what I said, McGrath," Adrian barked with no small amount of annoyance in his tone. "I'll arrange for some staff to handle housekeeping and provide meals, and set up computers and drafting areas for both architects. You'll have plenty of time to work and get a sense of the geography."

Three weeks. Alone. In a house with Gracie.

She shifted uncomfortably in her seat across the table. "That's quite a long time to be away from my office," she said slowly. "And you say the request is being made of another firm?"

Just then, she looked directly at him and her expression melted from confusion into horror.

Oh, yeah. *Three weeks. Alone. In a house with Gracie.*

His luck knew no bounds today. "Count me in, Adrian," he said pointedly into his phone, his gaze locked on the emerald eyes across from him. "You know I'll do what it takes to get the business."

The color drained from alabaster cheeks as Gracie pierced him with a glare. "Of course, Diane," she ground out. "Please tell Mr. Gilmore I'll do whatever is necessary."

They clicked off simultaneously.

"Well, what d'ya know, Gracie?" He reached over and playfully tapped her knife out of alignment. "There's going to be a future for us after all."

"Narragansett Bay scallops?"

Grace barely noticed the waiter standing next to the table as she closed the cover to her phone and dropped it into her jacket pocket.

Three weeks? In the carriage house? With him?

"For the lady," Colin said, that wicked smile still in place.

As the waiter set the dish in front of her, Grace was dimly aware of the aroma of pepper and parmesan. *Three weeks?*

"And the Portobello and gorgonzola sandwich," the waiter announced, positioning Colin's plate on the table.

The two men exchanged formalities about condiments, but Gracie didn't pay attention.

Three weeks?

There had to be some way to get out of this. But not if she wanted the Edgewater business. This arrangement was not negotiable. That much had been clear. Exactly *why* had not been clear at all.

"Is something the matter, ma'am?"

Grace looked up at the inquiring waiter. Yes. Indeed. Something was very much the matter. "No. This looks…perfect. Thank you."

Colin still wore that damn sly smile, and held her gaze with a look rich with humor and victory. "*Bon appetit,* Gracie."

She had no appetite, let alone a *bon* one.

She lifted her fork and let it clatter back down again. "Aren't we going to talk about this?"

"What's to talk about?" He scooped up his sandwich in his long fingers, gorgonzola cheese oozing from the bottom. "I get the impression from Adrian that it's a done deal."

"Adrian?" Her voice tripped.

"Yes. That was him on the phone. Who called you?"

Not Adrian, that's for sure. A bad sign. "His assistant, Diane," she admitted.

He gave her a "don't worry about it" expression that couldn't quite mask his pity. "No doubt he wanted to notify both firms simultaneously, so Diane helped."

Or he just plain liked Colin—and his *rule-breaking* ideas—better, and planned to give him the business after all. What if H&H had merely been included in this farce to make it look fair?

"I'm sure you're right," she agreed weakly, cutting a dainty piece of scallop.

He took a sizable bite from his sandwich, then put it down and touched his lips with the napkin.

She managed to spear her scallop with her fork, but couldn't quite lift it to her mouth. She watched him take a quick swipe of the bun with his tongue, catching some cheese. Her tummy did a tango at the sight.

The last thing she wanted Colin McGrath to know was how much the idea of three weeks alone with him unnerved her. Every instinct told her that he would relish that knowledge—and use it to his advantage.

"Eat some lunch, Gracie. The food's great." His eyes twinkled and he held out his gooey concoction toward her. "Want a bite of mine?"

The idea of putting her mouth where his had just been… Her breath caught in her already constricted throat.

"No, thank you." She finally slid a peppery scallop between her lips and chewed slowly. There. Did it. But could she swallow?

He put his sandwich down and wiped his mouth on the

linen napkin before taking a deep drink of water. Good God, the man ate with gusto. With perfectly acceptable manners, but so passionate.

"You don't think we'll have problems in such, uh, close quarters, do you, Gracie?" He was obviously holding back a laugh.

"Of course not," she lied. "Besides, the Edgewater carriage house is not exactly *close* quarters. I'll take the upstairs."

He raised both eyebrows. "The living area and kitchen are downstairs, if I recall the layout of the place. You'll need to eat and…live."

"I'll manage."

"And I'll need to sleep."

The scallop lodged and she coughed into her napkin. How was she going to get through this?

"Are you okay?" he asked, looking suitably concerned.

"Yes." She put her fork down and took a quick drink of water. "I'm fine."

He glanced at her still-full plate and raised an eyebrow. "I'm always a little suspicious of people who don't like to eat."

"I like to eat," she said defensively, lifting another bite to her mouth. "I just do things deliberately."

"I know."

Her dancing stomach did a low dip at that. "You do?"

He shrugged. "I remember you from college, Gracie."

She gave him a sharp look, and got a totally innocent one in return. "You know I was at CMU the whole time you were an undergrad," he continued. "I got my Masters while you were finishing college."

Did he think she hadn't seen him in the School of Architecture, in the halls, on the campus? Just because he didn't acknowledge her, and she responded in kind, didn't mean she wasn't painfully and totally *aware* of him. "Yes, I believe I knew that."

Suddenly, his expression turned solemn. "Gracie—"

She reached her fork across the table and stabbed a crispy French fry on his plate. "May I?"

"Of course." His grin was sheer delight.

At least her momentary lapse in manners made him stop before he said anything…about that night.

After a beat, he pushed his plate toward her. "Have all you like. Look, I know you've put these parameters up, but I want to tell you—"

"These are delicious." She lunged for another fry.

This time he laughed. "Okay. You win. I don't know you at all, I don't remember anything about you, and my years at CMU are a blur. Let's talk about the future."

Worse. "The next three weeks?"

"Yeah. Are we going to spend it avoiding a whole bunch of delicate subjects?"

She met his piercing gaze without wavering, wiping the corners of her mouth with the napkin. "Yes, we are. Here are the ground rules: We are going to avoid discussing our work, our ideas, our proposals, our companies, our past, our future and our present."

"It's gonna be a quiet house."

"A good working environment."

"I like loud rock music."

She blew out a breath. "I like soft classical."

"I sleep late."

"I get up and run at five-thirty every morning."

"I like take-out."

"I cook healthy food."

"You know what, Gracie?"

She brushed her hands against the linen napkin. "What, Colin?"

He grinned. "You're no fun."

"Thank you."

Laughing, he popped a French fry in his mouth and nodded slowly as he regarded her with a half smile. "And you've grown into quite a woman."

A rush of warmth spread through her. "Thank you, again."

He leaned over his plate and whispered, "I'm looking forward to the next three weeks."

"I'm looking forward to winning the Edgewater business," she said, holding his heated gaze.

"Maybe I could teach you a few things."

She arched a skeptical brow. "Like what?"

"Like how to enjoy loud music, late mornings, and takeout." He laughed softly and held up a French fry like a ketchupy peace offering. "And how to break some…ground rules."

Three

"**O**h my *Gawd*."

Grace twirled around to meet her roommate's stunned expression. "What's the matter, Allie?"

"I've never seen disorder in this room." Allie blinked sleepy brown eyes and pointed to Grace's bed. "I didn't think you knew how to make a mountain of discarded clothes. Have you run out of color-coded hangers?"

Grace gave her an imploring look. "Help me," she begged, hearing the note of panic in her own tone. "Gilmore gave us twenty-four hours to get back to Newport. I don't know what to take." She picked up a pair of jeans. "Do I pack for a vacation?" A suit jacket. "For work?" A skirt. "Is this trip some kind of a contest or is it—"

"Your every fantasy come true?" Allie reached into the pile and retrieved a slinky black dress, jiggling it seductively.

Grace grabbed the flimsy knit fabric and added it to the reject pile. "I don't know how you talked me into buying that. My only fantasy is to nail the Edgewater job."

"And as an added bonus, you may get to nail the competition."

Grace pointed her finger in her friend's face. "Allison Powers, you are a bad girl."

"I try. But, hey, *you* took me to his Web site last night to show off your new roommate." Allie flipped a strand of long black hair over her shoulder and sauntered around the bed, her Tweetie Bird slippers scuffing along the hardwood floor. "And I say, if you're ever ready to embrace the 'bad can be good' philosophy of life, now is definitely the time."

"Bad can never be good." Grace shook her head. "I'm not interested in casual sex with Colin McGrath. Remember? Been there, done that, regretted it for the rest of my life."

But she didn't regret her decision to confide the truth in Allie when she'd gotten home from Newport yesterday. She had to tell someone. And Allie had understood. After all, she'd been burned pretty badly herself, and much more recently.

Allie cleared some clothes and stretched out on Grace's bed. "I'm aware of your morals and I respect them. I might even embrace celibacy myself. But, sweetie, you're twenty-eight years old. Aren't you a little curious to find out what it's all about?"

"I'll find out what it's all about when I meet the one man who makes me feel whole and good and loved and worthy," Grace said vehemently. "When I do, I'll—I'll…"

"Nail him."

Grace smiled, and then leaned against the closet door to look at Allie. "It won't be like that."

"Don't expect hearts and flowers and violin music, darling," Allie lay back and rolled her eyes. "It ain't reality. And speaking of men who can't demonstrate their love, what did your dad say?"

Grace shook her head. "Why do I put up with you?"

"Because I keep you grounded and speak the truth."

That was for sure. Allie knew all about Grace's frustration with the Ice Man, Eugene Harrington. "I spoke with my dad this morning. He was hesitant, but then he talked to Adrian—"

"He *called* the client?"

"Yes," Grace admitted, the sting of it still smarting.

"That sucks," Allie said, curling comfortably on the bed. "He treats you like such a baby."

"That's why I have to win this project for the firm." Grace picked up a daring pink sweater Allie had given her for her twenty-eighth birthday. She held it out for a quick examination and dropped it. Too low, too tight. "I'm tired of being under his wing. This is my chance to soar."

Allie grabbed the discarded sweater and flung it over the clothes mountain into the open suitcase. "You'll soar with *that* on."

"Allie," Grace burned her with a look and left the sweater where it fell. "The last thing I need to do is mess up this opportunity by getting…involved with the competition."

"This has a lot less to do with the competition and a lot more to do with the effect that man has on you."

Right again. "You're imagining things."

"Oh, sure. Then why'd you have his Web site set as one of your 'favorite places'?" Allie jutted her chin toward something behind Grace's head. "Take that red sheath. You look fantabulous in that."

"This isn't about how I look." She pulled the dress from a hanger.

"Oh, really? Then why do I have the feeling that if you were sharing a honeymoon cottage with, oh, anyone else in the free world, that you would have your clothes neatly folded, separated by tissue, and alphabetically organized in your suitcase?"

So true. "It's a three-story house with at least five bedrooms. Not a honeymoon cottage."

"What*ever*. You know I'm right."

"Allie, Colin McGrath was my first big mistake in life. And, yes, I admit it. He's sinfully attractive. But that doesn't change how I feel about love and sex and the connection between the two. I could never love Colin McGrath."

"Why not?"

A tingling sensation started low in her stomach. "Because—he's, he's—because I…"

"You're scared of him."

She choked a futile denial.

"He could be that one man who gets to you."

She shook her head helplessly.

"You've never met anyone who spun you so out of control."

Why did Allie always have to be right?

Allie sat up and pointed her index finger accusingly. "You know what your problem is?"

"I think I'm about to find out."

"Honey, you're scared of a man who can show his feelings and get you to show yours. You've never let any guy get close to you—no doubt because of your crusty old man—and you don't know what to do when you're faced with one you might want."

"That may be true," Grace replied. "But Colin isn't the man for me. He's—he's rebellious and wild and irreverent and…and unorthodox."

Allie purred and tucked her Tweetie slippers under her. "Sounds divine."

"He took advantage of a woman who'd had five, maybe six, glasses of Southern Comfort, don't forget."

"You said it was mutual."

Grace bit back a dry laugh. "Oh, it was mutual." She'd thrown her arms around him in the dining room, kissing him first until they'd toppled to the ground for a few heated minutes of full body contact. That much she remembered. Then they'd grappled all the way up the stairs, his hands roaming her backside, her legs practically wrapped around his hips. Yep, she remembered that. Then they'd got to his room, and she didn't remember anything.

"But, Al, I was drunk for the first time in my life. Relieved of inhibitions and acting on the lustiest crush I'd ever known. He should have taken me home. Not upstairs to his room."

"Maybe he didn't think you were in any shape to go home," Allie suggested. "Maybe he was trying to make sure half the campus didn't see you blasted. Maybe he was protecting you."

"By having sex with me?"

Allie narrowed her eyes. "Are you absolutely certain you lost your virginity that night?"

With a decidedly unladylike snort, Grace shook her head. "Look, I woke up in his extra-large T-shirt and nothing else. *Someone* undressed me. And we were…intertwined." She flushed again at the memory of how hard he'd been against her, how their bodies had melded as if they belonged in that spoon position forever.

Forever?

"How did he act?"

"Weird."

"Weird?"

He'd been withdrawn, uncomfortable. Maybe a little embarrassed, too. "Well, he wasn't arrogant about his conquest. He denied anything happened."

"He did?" Allie propped her head up with interest. "Why would he lie?"

Colin McGrath never lies. The words of another architecture student still rang in her ears. But he must have. At least one time. "Probably so I wouldn't turn into a mad stalker. He wasn't interested in a girl like me. He liked—likes—wild, free-spirited things like himself. He was so sorry it ever happened. I could tell by the look on his face." It had been as cold as the damp clothes she'd found hanging in his shower. *What* had they done? "I just got the hell out of there as fast as possible."

"Was there blood from the grand de-flowering?"

Grace gave Allie a disgusted look. "I didn't inspect the sheets, Al. His room was a royal mess, I remember that. The guy's a slob. Anyway, not everyone bleeds, you know."

"Did it hurt? Were you sore?"

Sometimes Allie just went too far. "I believe the expression is 'feeling no pain,' Al. Yes, I was sore. My whole body felt like human train tracks."

"And did the morning express have a nice caboose?"

Grace folded the sleeves of a prim white cotton blouse and placed it carefully in her suitcase. "He has a nice everything, Allie. And I don't want to talk about it. He's the enemy. The competition. A demon with an earring and a ponytail."

Without a word, Allie eased herself off the bed, picked up the black dress, and held it poised over the suitcase. "Well, then, just in case you need to face some demons, Grace." She dropped it in. "Wear the right outfit."

"Good idea," Grace murmured.

After Allie left, she opened her top dresser drawer and took out one more item of clothing, one of her favorites. Without giving herself a chance to reconsider, she tucked it between the pink sweater and the black dress.

At the sight of Gracie's Audi parked in front of the carriage house, Colin's gut tightened in anticipation. Everything, in fact, had been pretty tight on him for the last twenty-four hours. An ice-cold swim at First Beach had helped, as had a sweaty run along Cliff Walk. But hunger and need had continued to gnaw at him since their lunch the day before.

He'd already made his decision about the weeks ahead.

He was no longer a blue-collar boy on a scholarship. He'd made his mark in the world, and he hadn't done it by lying back and letting life happen. Sure, he was lucky, as Gram said. The luckiest of the three McGrath brothers.

But he knew luck happened when you take chances and seize the day. And on this day, he had a second chance with the one woman whose memory had never left him. He was taking it. This time, his fantasies would come true. This time, he would make love to Gracie Harrington and she would enjoy and remember every minute.

After his run, he'd checked out of his hotel and shopped for a few items he'd need for the next three weeks—he'd only packed for two days and had no intention of driving back to Pittsburgh for more clothes. He arrived at the carriage house just a few minutes before five.

How long had she been there?

Grabbing his bags, he headed up the veranda steps, pausing on the porch to take the place in with a whole different eye. The glider suddenly looked like the perfect place to rock with Gracie, under a warm blanket. The chaise lounge in the yard could be a great place for catching a few rays, side by side.

And she could sit on his lap in that giant chair—

"You're late. Adrian said four o'clock."

Gracie stood in the entryway, in jeans and a creamy, cable-knit sweater, her hair pulled back in a ponytail, a challenge in her green eyes. He had to fight the impulse to reach out and touch her cheek.

How long could he fight his impulses? Let's see, it was Saturday at five. He could probably make it to, oh, nine that night. No. Maybe eight.

"I didn't know we had to punch a time clock."

She crossed her arms and glanced into the house for a second. "Who knows what the staff will report?"

"The staff?" A drop of disappointment trickled through him. "What staff?"

"Leonard Billingsly, our butler." She couldn't hide the

glimmer of satisfaction in her eyes. "He's veddy British and bakes a mean scone." Tapping the face of her watch, she added, "Which you missed because teatime was at four. Precisely."

"A butler?" Who lived in the house? In the middle of his fantasy?

At that moment, an older, heavyset man appeared in the entryway. "You must be Mr. McGrath," he said, his British accent noticeably more refined than Adrian Gilmore's.

Colin took the hand that was offered. "And you are Mr. Billingsly?"

"Correct, sir. Please call me Leonard. I am Mr. Gilmore's personal valet, but he's traveling for the next month and thought my services would be best put to use here, with you and Miss Harrington." He smiled at her, his bright blue eyes twinkling as he looked at her and she grinned back.

Great. Now he had to compete with the butler for her attention.

"I'll take those," Leonard offered, holding both hands out toward the shopping bags and his beat-up canvas suitcase, but Colin inched them back. No way he'd let a sixty-something guy carry his bags. Butler or not.

"Thanks, I got 'em." He indicated the door with a nod. "Just point me in the right direction."

And tell me my room is next to hers and a mile from yours.

"Certainly, sir. Allow me to escort you upstairs." Leonard glanced at Gracie before they all went inside. "I hope you enjoyed your tea, Miss Harrington. And the herb garden."

She smiled back at the older man, a picture of refinement. "I did, Leonard. Enormously. And you were absolutely right about that touch of nutmeg in the scones. A perfect complement to the peppermint tea."

Of course, Gracie felt right at home with a butler. And from the way ol' Lenny was beaming at her, he'd already fallen in love with Gracie, too.

Too?

Colin cleared his throat and took a step toward the door. "If you'll excuse me, I'll leave you two to exchange biscuit recipes."

Leonard ignored the comment and started up the stairs. "I've made up the west-facing guest suite for you. Miss Harrington indicated that she enjoys the morning light for early rising, and that you prefer, uh, a longer slumber."

Colin shot a quick narrow-eyed glance at Gracie as he passed her, which she responded to with an innocent shrug, and then he followed the butler up a massive set of stairs.

Although he wore a casual button-down shirt and dark pants, Leonard moved with well-trained grace, the epitome of a manservant. The very idea of a having a personal valet gave Colin the willies. He'd avoid this guy as much as humanly possible over the next three weeks.

"You should be quite comfortable here," the butler said, opening a door halfway down the hall.

Like all the rooms in the carriage house, this one was oversize and understated. The suite included a sitting area and full bath, all warmed by a long wall of arched windows that overlooked the water. "This is great," Colin said, tossing the bags on the bed. "Thanks."

"Would you like to see your studio, as well?" he asked.

Oh, yeah. He'd have to work while he was here. "Sure."

He followed Leonard up a back staircase at the end of the hall, which opened to a giant loftlike room that took the whole third floor.

"Mr. Gilmore built this studio last year when he was residing at Edgewater," Leonard told him. "He likes to paint in the magnificent light."

Somehow, he found it difficult to conjure up an image of Adrian Gilmore holding a palette and wearing a stained smock. But the studio rocked. With the late-afternoon sunlight pouring in the banks of windows along three walls, gleaming hardwood floors, and ten-foot ceilings, he could easily imagine wanting to spend hours here. *With Gracie.* At the far end, two matching drafting tables stood at opposing angles. Next to each, also arranged for privacy, were two state-of-the-art mirror-image workstations.

Someone had given this a great deal of thought. And someone had wired and furnished this artist's studio for *architects* in a remarkably short amount of time.

"This is awesome," he said, slowly crossing the room. "How'd you manage to get the drafting tables and computers set up in just one day?"

"Mr. Gilmore can accomplish anything he puts his mind to," Leonard assured him. "I assisted him in stocking the supplies. I've been instructed to make your stay as comfortable as possible, and to provide you with anything you need."

"That's great," Colin said, rubbing his chin. "We'll need some privacy. You know, a quiet work environment."

Leonard's lips curled up. "I am well trained to provide that, Mr. McGrath. I assure you, your working conditions will be ideal."

Colin was more concerned with the playing conditions. Better keep that to himself. Lenny had given his allegiance away with the nutmeg scones.

"I spend most of my time downstairs, Mr. McGrath," Leonard continued. "My quarters are attached to the kitchen, but you can reach me via the intercom system that Mr. Gilmore had installed."

"Sounds like Adrian spent more time in the carriage house than he did at Edgewater," Colin noted.

"Mr. Gilmore entertained on occasion at the mansion before the fire, but, yes, he was more comfortable in the smaller environs of this home."

Which would bode well for the Pineapple House plans.

"How often did he entertain at the mansion?" Colin asked.

Gracie answered from the studio door. "Often enough to want it rebuilt."

He laughed and waved her in. "Nice digs, huh, Gracie?"

"I can get a lot of work done in here," she agreed, taking a step farther into the room. "I'll take mornings. You can have afternoons."

He raised his eyebrows. "That's not necessary. I swear I won't peek at your work."

"Not a chance." She pointed to a sleek sound system built into a wall unit. "I can't stand loud music."

He wasn't about to try and persuade her in front of the help. There would be plenty of time for persuasion. "We'll figure something out."

"You can do that over dinner," Leonard said. "Cocktails are at six on the veranda."

"Just iced tea for me," Gracie said.

"Of course, Miss Harrington," he agreed. "Supper can be in the dining room, or al fresco in the back courtyard, the choice is yours."

"In the courtyard," Colin said.

"In the dining room," Grace said at the same time.

Leonard barely hid his chuckle as he moved toward the door. "You can tell me once you've decided. I'll be in the kitchen."

When he was gone, they stood in a moment of awkward silence. Gracie crossed the room toward the workstations, the light glancing off her shiny hair, her figure silhouetted in the window. Colin wanted to stare at her, to appreciate the way the sun warmed her creamy complexion, to examine the way her sweater clung to feminine curves and to memorize the way her jeans hugged her narrow hips.

Another impulse he had to fight. Drinking in Gracie.

"Pretty amazing that Gilmore pulled this off in one day,

don't you think?" he asked. "In fact, it looks like he's been cooking up this shoot-out all along."

She jerked her head up from the drafting table she'd been inspecting. "What do you mean?"

"I don't know." He shrugged and approached her. "Setting up CAD systems, tables…" He scooped up a handful of acrylic pencils from the opposing table. "My favorite brand, my favorite colors."

She frowned and shrugged. "That's a popular brand, and—" she raised her eyebrows and examined the pencils "—nothing too risky here, colorwise."

He fought a smile at the little dig. "And on your desk?"

She lifted a box of lead colored pencils. "I don't use acrylic. Not precise enough."

"Almost as though he was prepared for us. Or for somebody."

"I suppose it's possible he knew there would be finalists," she said, fluttering some tracing paper on the desk. "But he couldn't have known ahead of time who they'd be. These are typical architect tools. Leonard went to an office supply store and asked for what architects use." She glanced at his acrylics. "Good architects."

He laughed, fighting one more impulse—this one to bury his face in her hair and inhale the subtle floral scent that clung to her. Was it lavender? Gardenia? "You're probably right."

She moved away, tapping her drafting table. "I like this one, and not just because my favorite type of isograph pen was already here. I like the view."

He glanced behind her to the scenery out the window. "You like looking at a barbecued replica of Buckingham Palace?"

"I find it inspiring to know I'll be designing its replacement."

"Good, because this—" he pointed to the area on the south side of the building "—is the perfect view for me."

She moved next to him. "Why? That was the old side yard. Nothing spectacular, unless you like croquet."

"Everything spectacular, in my opinion," he said, draping a casual arm around her shoulder and gently tugging her into his side. She stiffened, but stayed there. "That was where Pineapple House once stood." He leaned closer. Lavender. Definitely. He held out his hand to direct her gaze. "Use your imagination. Just picture it. All clean lines, perfect proportions, and classic eighteenth-century architecture."

He glanced down at her. Her gaze was focused on the grounds, no doubt using her architect's vision.

"I would really love to see the records of that building," she said, and then quickly added, "Just out of professional curiosity, naturally."

When she looked up at him, his heart twisted. Why did Gracie affect him this way? He lowered his voice to an inviting whisper. "Have dinner with me under the stars and I'll share them with you."

Her defiant look softened, as did the color of her grass-green eyes, and she didn't pull away or break their gaze. *Say yes, Gracie.*

"Colin, for the sake of propriety and sanity over the next three weeks, do you think we could manage to keep this as platonic as possible?" she asked.

He had no use for propriety or sanity. And forget platonic, at least where Gracie was concerned. "No."

Her lips formed a tiny little O of surprise. This time, he couldn't fight the impulse. He dipped his head and kissed her beautiful mouth.

Her lips were warm and tangy with the taste of peppermint tea. He slid the tip of his tongue against her lips, the sensation of intimacy sending a lightning bolt of pleasure through him. Her mouth was soft and supple, causing a sudden ache to pull at him head to toe, and one very specific place in between. His desire was instant—and powerful.

He wrapped his other arm around her waist, pulling the

curve of her woman's body against him. Her heart hammered with the same rhythm as his, and a secret moan vibrated in her throat just as she gathered a handful of his sweatshirt in her fist. He wasn't sure if she was going to slug him, shove him across the room, or yank him in for a closer inspection.

She did none of those things. She shuddered and inched away, shaking her head slowly as though she could will her brain to *behave.* For some reason, that made him want to laugh. But he didn't.

"Some things are just too powerful to fight, Gracie."

She responded with a flash of green eyes. "Well, you better start fighting. For twenty-one days."

He smoothed her hair, his fingers lingering against the silk of her cheek. "I can think of worse ways to spend three weeks. But we can take things at whatever speed you want."

She managed to escape his touch. "Zero. That's the speed I'm interested in. No speed and no 'things.'"

"You really don't like to lose control, do you, Gracie?"

With a deep breath, she shook her head again. "Losing control has never worked out well for me." He saw her throat move as she struggled to swallow. "As you know."

"Gracie—"

She held up a hand to his face. "Colin, please understand this. History is not going to repeat itself."

He choked out a quick laugh. "I don't think you know what you're saying."

"I know exactly what I'm saying," she insisted. "Maybe for one crazy second there, I didn't know what I was *doing,* but I know what I'm saying. I won't make that mistake again."

The time had come to end this stupid misconception and get Gracie to feel something other than contempt for him. It was one thing for her to hate him because he wasn't in her social stratosphere. But he wouldn't go another minute with her thinking he'd had his way with a drunken eighteen-year-old. "Gracie, listen to me."

She didn't say anything, but crossed her arms, backing up as she held his gaze. "I'm listening."

"I know a whole bunch of time has gone by and you're a grown woman, so this really doesn't matter anymore, but I want to clear something up once and for all."

He took a step closer and put both hands on her shoulders, and she lifted her chin to him. "Fine, say it," she ground out. "I am a grown woman, so I'm mature enough to accept your apology."

Apology? "I'm not going to apologize for anything."

A pink stain spread on her cheeks. "Of course not. Who would expect you to? Should I apologize for throwing myself at you?" She tried to wriggle her shoulders out of his grasp, but he held firmly. "You're a jerk, you know that?"

He tightened his grip and lowered his voice. "Gracie, I didn't have sex with you."

Everything stopped. The energy that vibrated between them, the jerky movement of her body, even her breathing. All stopped.

"You're lying."

"I don't lie, Gracie. I'm not capable of it."

She just stared at him.

"You were sick, really, really sick, when we got to my room. And you passed out on the bathroom floor."

She cringed, then frowned in confusion. "Why didn't you tell me that?"

"I tried," he said with an exasperated breath. "You were in no mood to listen, if you remember. All you wanted to do was get the hell out of there."

"You—you undressed me because I was sick?"

He nodded. "Your clothes were a wreck. You—you reeked. I couldn't take you home like that. There were still about forty people roaming around downstairs."

"And you didn't…?"

"*No.* I didn't." He gave into a sneaky smile. "Okay, I looked. I mean, I undressed you, cleaned you up, but that's all. But you were out cold. I wanted you…clearheaded. I wanted you to feel the same way I did."

The same way I do.

As quickly as the color rose in her cheeks, it faded to a bloodless white. "You mean… all this time, I thought I lost…"

"As much as I would have loved to have the honor, Gracie, I wasn't your first. All I did was…" He paused and rubbed her shoulders gently, the way he had that night. "I just stayed awake and watched you. To make sure you didn't get sick any more in your sleep. People die like that, you know."

Still she stared at him, her mouth open. He finally took his finger and tapped her jaw up. "See that? You didn't even know it when you did lose your virginity."

"But I haven't," she said simply.

This time, *he* stopped breathing. He couldn't have understood that correctly. "Excuse me?"

She let out a self-conscious laugh. "I've never had another drink, either. And if you're telling the truth, I haven't…you know."

She…*hadn't?* Was it possible Gracie was a *virgin?*

His immediate reaction was so strong, it felt like a punch. *He wanted to be her first.* An unfamiliar euphoria erupted in his chest just as a glint he'd never seen before lit her eyes. Could she be thinking the same thing?

She laid a hand on her own chest and shook her head slightly. "You have no idea what a gift you've given back to me."

"A gift?" He heard the tightness in his voice.

Her fingers fluttered self-consciously. "I know this sounds kind of old-fashioned, but I've always wished I could have given my virginity to someone I love."

Her words flattened his fantasies like a bulldozer. "That's…noble," he managed.

The sparkle in her eyes turned into a full-blown glisten. No. A tear. "Now I can give myself to the man I fall in love with."

"Yes, you can," he whispered, a twinge of flat-out jealousy replacing his short-lived ecstasy. "And he'll be one helluva lucky guy."

But *his* luck had just run out. Because even if he had any desire or inclination to fall into that black pit of trouble, he was the last man on earth Grace Harrington would ever love.

Four

Grace flipped the eyelet comforter off her, surrendering to sleeplessness. Even opening one of the windows to let in the salty, September air didn't make her sleepy. What was wrong with her?

Hunger. Of course. She'd skipped dinner and that emptiness in the pit of her stomach was the need for food. The glow-in-the-dark hands of her travel clock pointed almost straight up. It was only a few minutes past midnight. She had a long, sleepless, hungry night ahead of her.

It had been a little childish to forego dinner, and she knew it. But Colin had suddenly disappeared, telling Leonard that he would be having dinner in town with a friend—he had a friend in Newport?—and Grace had declined the butler's offer to make her the blackened salmon he'd been planning to prepare.

What was she going to do, sit out on the patio and eat alone by candlelight? Leonard wouldn't have joined her even if she'd asked. He was a by-the-book butler, that was for sure.

For a moment she thought of Hannah, the housekeeper who'd practically raised her. Miss Hannah would certainly eat with her; she'd never let Grace eat alone. In fact, she had kept Grace company on many a night in the empty Harrington house.

Her feet hit the wood floor with a thud. There was no way she'd just lie here and think. She didn't relish the thought of raiding Leonard's pantry this late at night, but maybe she could scare up a cup of tea or glass of milk. She'd find something in that vast country kitchen.

The hallway outside her room was lit by one tiny lamp on a table at the far end. There were two closed doors—one was Colin's room. The other was another guest room. Her bare feet made no noise on the long Oriental runner in the hall, but the second step squeaked on the massive staircase. She paused, waiting for the sound of a door to open upstairs, but the house stayed silent.

In the kitchen, she noticed the door to the back rooms was closed, but light could seep underneath and wake Leonard up. Right now, she didn't want any company or help, so she simply popped the refrigerator door a little and peered in.

What was that on the second shelf? She slid the dish closer and saw the cherries mixed into the creamy frosting. Black Forest cake. She stifled a moan of delight.

But it was just too decadent to eat cake in the middle of the night. Tea would do the trick.

In a cabinet, she found some Earl Grey tea in an unopened box. Did Earl Grey have caffeine? She didn't want a boost of energy—just the opposite. The label didn't mention caffeine and the idea of a cup of tea was so inviting, she decided to take a chance.

Even though the moonlight that poured through the window over the sink offered enough light, she couldn't find the tea kettle. Leonard ran a shipshape kitchen, which she appreciated, but she had to settle for heating water in a saucepan.

She was sure she could figure out the microwave, but the beep might wake up Leonard...or Colin. She glanced down at her flimsy tank top and sleep pants. Nope, she certainly didn't want Colin's company.

The idea sent a little zing through her and she just shook her head as she cut a lemon for the tea. How long could she lie to him—and to herself? How long could she act cool and unresponsive? The man did things to her. He electrified her. He jangled every nerve ending in her body and sent pulsating shockwaves to places...that she had effectively deadened for most of her adult life. And he did something else.

He made her doubt her decision.

For the first time in ten years, Gracie wondered exactly *why* she was so determined to hold on to her virginity.

Refusing to examine the thought further, she took her tea into the living room, but the autumn air called to her. Grabbing an afghan from the back of the living-room sofa, she slipped out the front door to the veranda.

Perfect. Ocean air and Earl Grey tea. This would surely make her sleepy. She lifted the cup from her saucer to her mouth, inhaling the citrusy aroma of the fresh-cut lemon.

"Are you all alone?"

The china bumped her front tooth, but she managed to avoid spilling the tea at the sound of a voice from the lawn. Not just any voice. Colin's voice.

She peered into the darkness. "Where are you?"

A shadow moved near a cluster of evergreens on the side of the carriage house. "I'm right here," he said, the sound closer. Suddenly she could see him in the moonlight, at the bottom of the veranda steps.

"What are you doing out here?" she asked, pulling the afghan a little tighter over her pajamas.

"I live here, remember?"

"I mean out, at night."

"I'm a big boy," he laughed and took the first few steps up. "I was in town. What are you doing up so late? Surely you have to rise and run in a matter of a few hours."

"I can't sleep, so I decided to have some Earl Grey tea. Would you like me to make you some?"

In the dim light, she saw a wry smile tip his lips. "No thanks. I just had a Sam Adams at the Black Pearl. I never mix Earl and Sam."

She smiled at the joke, but wondered just who he'd been drinking his beer with. "I thought you were asleep."

He shrugged and approached the glider. "Nah. I'm a certified night owl. Can I join you?"

She scooted into the farthest corner of the glider, and he dropped right into the middle, leaving the whole left side open. The seat rocked a little under his body weight.

He wore jeans and a dark sweatshirt. As he sat down, Grace noticed that his hair wasn't tied back. For a minute, she stared at the sight it made, falling to his shoulders, straight and black as the sky. Utterly beautiful. Utterly touchable.

She turned her full attention to the tea.

He put his arm across the back, and extended his long legs in front of him. She closed her eyes and sipped.

"It can't be a guilty conscience keeping you awake," he said.

She opened her eyes. "Pardon me?"

"My Gram says a guilty conscience keeps a good man awake. Or woman, in this case. But since you've been absolved from a sin you never committed, that can't be what's causing your insomnia."

She shot him a warning look. "Do you think we can just drop that subject for the next, oh, three weeks?"

With a soft chuckle, he crossed his ankles and she could still feel him looking at her. Defiantly, she took her swallow of tea. Neither said anything for a minute, the night sounds of the crickets and an ocean breeze rustling in the dry, autumn leaves enough to fill the silence.

"What did Lenny make you for dinner?"

"Lenny?" She almost choked on the tea. *"Lenny?"*

"Mr. Billingsly, my dear. Our esteemed valet."

She laughed at his fake English accent. "I didn't eat. But don't make fun of a man who can bake a Black Forest cake. I saw it in the fridge."

He shifted closer and she could feel the weight of his hand and arm at the nape of her neck. "Why didn't you eat dinner?"

She refused to admit it was too lonely without him. "I was busy. Making calls. Checking things in the office."

"Alerting the media of your news?"

This time she seared him with a full-on dirty look. "Of course. I had to get it in the *Boston Globe.*"

His soft laugh reverberated across the grounds.

"Shhhh." She tapped his arm and stole another peek at his hair when he wasn't looking. God, it was…inviting. Her fingers literally ached to touch it. "Don't wake up…*Lenny.*"

He caught her gaze. "What are you looking at, Gracie?"

She felt the heat rise in her cheeks, and blessed the dim light. "I've never seen your hair down," she admitted.

He reached back and lifted a handful, then let it drop. "The tie fell out tonight."

An unwelcome sensation of dread rolled through her. What was he doing at the Black Pearl that his hair came *undone?*

"So who'd you have dinner with?" she asked casually, taking a tiny sip of tea.

His fingertips brushed her own hair where it hit the back of the glider. "A close friend of mine."

She remembered his friends from college. Edgy, artistic, experimental. She remembered the time she'd seen him with a raven-haired freshman on the back of his motorcycle near campus. To this day, she remembered the sinking feeling of inadequacy when she saw the girl wrap her arms possessively around Colin's waist, and lay her head against his back. With no helmet, naturally. A wild, uninhibited girl. Grace had been overcome with a longing so sharp, it hurt.

"You have a friend who lives locally?"

"A native Newporter actually. She knows a lot about the history of the town."

She. The tea caught in her throat, but Grace asked casually, "So what did you learn about the history of Newport?"

He moved his feet in a slow rhythm, easing the glider into a steady rock. "We were talking about Rejects Beach."

"Rejects Beach? Isn't that what they call that area right over there by Ledge Road? Where Cliff Walk begins?"

He nodded. "Yeah. All of Bailey's Beach used to be private, part of the country club and exclusively for the wealthiest residents of Newport. But the eastern end kept getting invaded by the unwashed public, so the highbrows erected a fence."

She couldn't help noting the bit of disdain in his voice, but drank the rest of her tea without commenting while he told her the story of how a group of radical locals fought for the fence to be taken down and eventually won.

"They got their way, but the area was branded 'Rejects Beach' by the members of the private club at the other end of Bailey's Beach. Even now, the tennis and polo crowd takes a dim view of the riffraff who darken their sand."

She adjusted the blanket and started to stand.

"Where are you going, Gracie?"

"To wash my cup and saucer."

He shook his head and took the dishes from her hand. "Here." In one movement, he unceremoniously set the two pieces of fine china on the wooden floor next to him with a little clatter. "Do it later. Stay here with me."

A splash of anticipation tickled the very nerve endings

she'd been thinking about in the kitchen. She smoothed the edges of the blanket and tucked her bare feet under her.

And Colin moved at least six inches closer.

For one insane moment her stomach swayed, but the glider didn't. She studied his face in the moonlight as he looked out over the grounds, noticing his stubble of whiskers was darker than usual. He hadn't shaved before going out with "his friend."

Had he kissed this local girl? Shared his beer with her? What would those whiskers feel like if he kissed her?

She turned away and looked into the shadows. Good God, how was she going to get through three weeks if her every other thought with him included the word *kiss?*

"I really ought to get to sleep soon if I'm going to get any work done in the morning," she said feebly. But she didn't want to leave this glider or end this moment.

"Don't worry. Tomorrow's Sunday. You can have the studio all day if you want it."

"What will you do?"

He shrugged. "Haven't decided yet. I don't have any agenda. Do you have any plans?"

"Nothing you'd be interested in, I assure you."

"Try me."

"I'll work, then I'm planning to tour some of the mansions."

"Which ones?"

"I was thinking I'd visit the Breakers and Rosecliff just to soak up the ambiance. They have some similarities to Edgewater, especially in the way they are situated on the property. And it's been a few years since I've been inside the Elms. Even though that's not a waterfront mansion, it is comparable to Edgewater."

He rocked the glider again, his arm draped across the back, even closer to her. "You should go to Hunter House."

"Why would I do that?" she asked.

"Hunter House is an excellent example of Georgian colonial architecture from the mid-eighteenth century. Besides giving you an understanding of what the competition is presenting, you should just experience it. Just for the pure pleasure of it."

"I'm not interested in Georgian colonial architecture from the mid-eighteenth century," she said, pulling the blanket tighter. "I don't need to experience anything just for pure pleasure."

His laugh was low and rich with irony. "Evidently." He lifted a strand of hair and let it flutter back over her neck. "But needing and wanting are two different things."

Speaking of pure pleasure.

She shifted away from him and curled deeper into her corner. "Don't tease me, Colin."

He gave his head a slow, negative shake. "No can do, Gracie. It's too much fun."

Fun for him. "I can't get through the next three weeks if you constantly bring up the subject of…what I'm missing."

"You're missing Georgian architecture, that's all."

She shot him a warning look. "You know what I mean. Everything you say is loaded with…double meaning."

"You're imagining things," he denied with a laugh. "But I'll make you a deal. I'll promise to speak with one, straightforward meaning if you'll make me a promise, too."

She started to agree, then caught herself. "That depends on what you ask."

"Every single day you're here, you will break one rule."

"Excuse me?"

"Just something little. Take a risk, break a rule. Like putting your dishes on the floor for twenty minutes instead of running into the kitchen to wash them."

Those kinds of rules she could break. But what else did he have in mind? "I don't know," she said, with a slow smile. "I don't want to compromise my standards."

He ruffled her hair again, sending a cascade of tingles down her back. "You don't have to compromise anything, Gracie. I just want to see you have a little fun."

This was fun, she realized with a start. Being this close to Colin McGrath, sitting in the moonlight, inhaling his masculine scent, watching that tiny gold ring in his ear move with each tip of the glider. This was just plain, unadulterated fun.

"I don't know," she said. "I like rules."

"It's all about control, and you're an expert there." Somehow, he'd moved all the way over to her side of the glider and now sat just inches from her. "As long as you maintain control, rules can be broken. That's how I approach architecture."

"That's how you approach life."

He grinned. "Watch out. It's contagious."

That's what she was worried about. "All right. One rule a day. Starting tomorrow. But no more double entendres thick with…implications."

"Deal. But not starting tomorrow. It's after midnight, so let's start right now." He closed the space between them, slowly lifting the edge of the blanket. "What are you wearing?"

Grace tried to swallow. "Pajamas."

"Then you'll need to change."

"Why?"

"We're going for a walk."

"Now? Where?"

"Cliff Walk."

"Cliff Walk?" She almost laughed at the absurd idea. "You can't go out there at night. I'm sure it's against the law."

He grinned and stood up, holding his hand to her. "Precisely why we're going there."

"It gets a little tricky at Ledge Road," Colin warned. Gracie paused in the driveway, but he tugged her farther away from the safety of the carriage house. "You're serious about Cliff Walk at this time of night?"

"Of course. Trust me, it's amazing at night. You can see the moon over the whole of Rhode Island Sound and absolutely no one is around."

"Which is exactly why it's a bad idea." She yanked up the zipper of the jacket she'd pulled over her jeans and sneakers. She'd had a hard time in her room for the last fifteen minutes, but had effectively managed to rationalize a moonlight stroll with Colin McGrath. Some of her courage faded in the dark, however. "A person could get killed out there at night."

He draped a casual arm over her shoulder, steering her toward the road. "I ran the entire three and a half miles yesterday morning. There are a few rugged spots on the southern half, but I won't let you get hurt, Gracie."

She knew the trail fairly well, too. Well enough to know that the "rugged" parts—basically where Bellevue met Ledge Road and the historic path started—were difficult to navigate even in broad daylight. The rocks could be slippery, and some of the first few drops were fairly steep until the path smoothed out.

"Why don't we just cruise the Edgewater property and you can show me where you're going to put Pineapple House?"

He stopped and gave her an incredulous look before breaking into a huge grin. "That's what I call positive thinking, Gracie."

"I—I meant where you *propose* to situate Pineapple House," she backtracked, trying not to be further distracted by his handsome white smile against tanned skin.

He tugged her closer into his side, the solid strength of him warming right through the fleece of her jersey. "I'll show you that tomorrow, in the light. Tonight, I want to walk with you."

It seemed innocent enough—a late-night walk in the brisk September air. Since he wasn't working in the studio tomorrow, she'd already decided to sleep in a little. Plus, something had her jittery. Maybe the Earl Grey tea had had caffeine, after all.

As he guided her through the gate that led to a wide shelf of smooth stone, she could hear the surf smash rhythmically against the rocky shoreline far below. The three-quarter moon peeked out from a thin cloud, providing light, but not really enough when she considered the uneven rocks just a few feet ahead.

"Don't let go of my hand," he said, taking hers as they crossed the first section of the eroded path.

She wouldn't dream of it. "Just don't go sliding way down…" she tilted her head toward the cliff's edge "…there."

"I won't. I'm in control," he said, a little wry humor coloring his voice.

They walked for a few minutes without any more conversation, allowing Grace to concentrate on each critical footstep. But her focus kept returning to the strong, large hand that engulfed hers. And the sheer proximity of one very masculine man on one very dangerous cliff. She took a deep breath to keep her balance. And, of course, control.

"There's Rejects Beach," he said, looking out toward the shore beyond the cliffs.

As he reached the end of the rocky area, he stepped in front of her, jumped down about a foot and turned around to help her. Putting his hands on her waist, he easily guided her to the safety of the traditional path.

"Here we go. The riskiest part is over." It was wider now, with a high rocky cliff on one side, and a low, protective railing along the long drop to the beach. Still, his fingers lingered a moment on her waist, his face a few inches from hers. Her heart did a sudden flutter and she realized that maybe the riskiest part of the walk was still ahead.

When they had their footing, he looked toward the eastern

end of Bailey's Beach, still holding her hand. "Rejects Beach is just another example of the vast separation of the rich and the common man that colors the history of this harbor."

This wasn't the first time she could hear the passion in his voice on this subject. She'd heard it in the restaurant when he'd revealed his plans. "Don't tell me. You see Pineapple House as a celebration of the common man."

His grip on her fingers tightened ever so slightly as she waited for his response. Although there was no more immediate danger on this walk, the feel of his hand was too warm, too comforting to pull away now.

"I see Pineapple House as a celebration of the roots of Newport, which, as a matter of fact, are quite common and had nothing to do with the ridiculous wealth that eventually overtook the place."

She'd expected a different response altogether. "I thought you'd launch into some speech about the intrinsic beauty of eighteenth-century architecture and the need to balance the heritage of the blah blah blah…"

"Blah blah *blah?*" He tried to sound indignant, but his laugh broke through the quiet of the night. "That's what you think of my brilliant and radical ideas?"

"Who cares what I think when you have *Newsweek* asking, 'Is the world ready for the avant-garde genius of Colin McGrath?'"

"I care what you think." The words, stated so simply, had the same effect as a dropping elevator. "And, frankly, I'm surprised you read that article, considering…our history."

Read it? She'd bought it the day it hit the stands. "Oh, I, uh, picked it up in the employee break room."

"That article was a bunch of BS, didn't you think so?"

"Not really." She didn't think that at all when she'd cut out the single page and stored it in the bottom of her jewelry box. "I thought it was good press coverage."

He squeezed her hand playfully. "You're lying."

"Okay. You got me. I thought, 'Wow. I didn't even know they liked opera in Portland.'"

His laugh was quick, but his expression grew serious again. "I bet you read it and thought, 'Oh, there's the schmuck who snagged me in college.'"

She looked up at him. Was that remorse in his voice? His eyes were teasing her, but he wasn't smiling. Unable to stop herself, her gaze dropped to his mouth. He was so close, so kissably close. Grace had to stop herself from lifting up on her toes and placing her lips on his.

With one finger under her chin, he raised her face to his, bringing her so near to him that she could already imagine what he'd taste and feel like.

"Tell me the truth," he said. "What did you think when you read that article?"

She'd thought that she still had a crush so deep and profound that just looking at his picture made her heart ache. And looking at the real man—with the spidery shadows of his eyelashes that the moonlight cast over his cheeks and the faint dark stubble in the hollows of his cheeks—made her ache all over again.

Her crush was as deep as ever.

But she'd had another emotion when she'd read that article, one that was safe, if not flattering, to admit. "I was jealous."

"Jealous?" He inched back enough to give her a look of utter disbelief. "Of a little press coverage?"

"Of your ability to buck the trends and make it work. That structure was breathtaking and you know it."

"Wow." He dipped just a fraction of an inch closer. Perilously close. How could she stop herself from kissing him? *How?* "That's quite a compliment from you, Miss Harrington."

"I recognize good work. Even if it is…risky." She tried to take a breath, but couldn't. She could practically feel her brain shutting down as her physical response to him took over.

"Be very careful, Gracie." His warning was delivered in a hushed, husky voice. "Once you live life without rules, you might not be able to stop."

I'll take that chance. Wordlessly, she rose up and covered his mouth with hers. He drew her into him, parting his lips and tilting his head. His warm, silky tongue glided into her mouth, sending a shower of sparks straight through her.

She heard her own low throaty response as her arms wrapped around his neck and she could finally, finally bury her fingers into the glossy strands of his hair.

With each exchange of their tongues, with each increase of pressure against her stomach and breasts, a melty feeling threatened her stability, turning her legs into rubber and creating a whirlpool of wild vibrations deep inside her. Through the sweatshirt, she could feel the steady thump of his heart as his whole being hardened in response to her.

Slowly, agonizingly, he ended the kiss.

"Gracie," he whispered into her mouth.

He pulled farther back, breaking the connection of searing heat that had formed between them.

She tried to say something but that shaky, needy feeling nearly obliterated her ability to speak. "I—I just—"

"Shh." He put one finger on her lips and she considered opening her mouth just to—lick his finger. God, was she *insane?*

The thought made her jerk backward and he grabbed her sweatshirt before she actually touched the guardrail. "Hey, hey, careful," he said, pulling her back. "Remember. Control is everything, Gracie."

Control. Yes. Right. She'd had that, once.

She inched backward, aware of the dangerous drop behind her, but far more terrified of the granite-hard man in front of her. Once again she was standing between two treacherous alternatives. She gave him an unsteady smile. "I'm fine," she tried to reassure him. And herself.

"I'll say." He matched her half smile. "That was an excellent demonstration of rule breaking." Then he turned them in the direction they'd come, a glimmer of regret in his expression. "But I think we've pushed your limit for today."

"No."

He halted midstep. "No?"

"I have one more rule to break."

He let out another one of those sexy, teasing laughs. "What d'ya have in mind, honey?"

"You'll see."

Before he responded, she took off in a slow jog toward the gate.

Five

"**M**mm." Gracie closed her eyes as a soft, sensual moan escaped her lips. "The man is truly gifted."

She slowly drew the chocolate-covered fork from her mouth, her delicate tongue dabbing at a tiny crumb of Black Forest cake that clung to her lips. Colin simply stared, slack-jawed and in wonder, his own piece of cake untouched on the plate in front of him.

Suddenly her eyes popped open and he knew he was busted. Staring, gawking, gaping. But certainly not eating.

"Aren't you even going to taste it? It's out of this world."

He leaned on the country kitchen table and propped his chin on his knuckles. "Watching you eat chocolate is about as far out of this world as I want to go."

"You're crazy." Her eyes sparkled as she opened her sweet mouth for another bite. "This, my friend, is a work of art."

He didn't know which he liked more—her lips pursed around a fork, or being her friend. "It's too rich for me."

"Oh, God, just have one bite." She gingerly slid her fork between the layers of cake, filling its tines with creamy chocolate. She held up the fork to his mouth, and then jerked it back, flicking the edge with her tongue. "Control, remember?" She grinned just before she ate it.

Of course he remembered. He'd dug deep for every ounce of control he could muster out on Cliff Walk half an hour ago, and had barely come up with a handful of the stuff. But how long would it last? Gracie was the most tempting woman he could remember who continually surprised him and easily aroused him.

Control—never his strong suit, despite his claims— would be his constant companion for three weeks. That and the icy-cold waters of First Beach. That would be the only way to get through this without making a total fool of himself. But what about all the hours they'd spend together during Adrian's little experiment? More meals, more walks, more mouth-to-mouth. How much control was a guy expected to exert?

He shifted in his chair. "What if Lenny's a spy?"

She looked at him questioningly, but didn't answer, her mouth busy with her last bite.

"Really, Gracie. What if he's Adrian Gilmore's plant to make sure his plan is working?"

She swallowed and dabbed her mouth with a paper napkin. "He'll know his plan worked when we present our final ideas in three weeks," she said. "No big mystery there."

"Maybe. Maybe not."

"What are you getting at? Do you still think this whole thing is some elaborate scheme that he'd planned?"

"I think that's worth considering."

"So what if it is?" She stood and took her empty dish to the sink, where she'd left her teacup and saucer—*unwashed*—

when they'd left for their walk. He considered it a small victory. "We're the firms he picked, so it really doesn't matter."

He idly pushed his plate away, not the least interested in eating the cake. Unless it was from Gracie's mouth. Now that held some serious appeal.

"Sure," he agreed. "We duke it out at the final presentation, but why us? Why alone? Why here?"

She turned from the sink. "Why not? We're the best there is."

"Why not, say, someone else from H&H?"

He watched the glow fade from her expression. "You, too, huh?"

"What do you mean?"

She stepped over to the table and picked up his plate. "Are you finished?"

"You want that piece, too?"

With an exasperated look, she added it to the pile in the sink. "You have no idea how hard I had to fight to get this assignment and everyone at my firm thinks it was handed to me on a silver platter, one that had my *family* name engraved on it." She flipped the faucet with a jerk. "Even my father doesn't think I can really handle it."

He had no doubt her colleagues cried nepotism, but her father? Her father thought the sun, the moon and all the stars were placed in the sky for the sole purpose of shining light on his Grace. That much was obvious from one conversation with the guy.

"Screw your co-workers," he said, more willing to address that issue than the one of her father. "They're just jealous because you're talented and beautiful and you're going to be their boss someday."

Her hands stilled under the running water, then she finished rinsing the plate she held. "Thank you for the compliments." Her voice was noticeably tighter than when she was singing

Lenny's culinary praises. "If I am their boss, I want to earn the privilege, not have it handed to me."

"And I'm sure you will." He reached over and took the clean, wet plate from her hand and wrapped it in a kitchen towel.

"I will if I win this bid."

Somehow he managed not to drop the expensive piece of china he held. Dabbing at the delicate pattern, he paused to swallow the myriad of cynical retorts that rose up. "I guess that's one way to squash a guy's enthusiasm for the job."

She pushed a strand of blond hair away from her cheek with her wrist and glanced at him. "Come on. You thrive on competition, Colin."

"Competition, yes." Opening the glass door of an antique china cabinet, he set the plate on top of a pile of others. "Career derailment, no."

When he turned back, she was holding out the next plate for him to dry. Funny how fast a couple formed a domestic assembly line in the kitchen. Well. Two *people*. Not exactly a *couple*.

"My career is not yours to derail," she said, sincerity and determination darkening her eyes. "I just have to win the bid and then it will be a nonissue."

"But I'm going to win this bid." Of that, he had no doubt. Someone else's happiness hinged on it; someone he owed a great deal to. He wouldn't dream of failure.

"You go on thinking that, McGrath." Her voice was light, confident. Of course. She had no idea that this was more than a pure business challenge to him. "In fact, you sleep on that until late tomorrow morning. By then, I should have my first-floor elevation finished."

But *he* was going to win this bid.

And then he'd be part of another huge and life-changing disappointment for Gracie Harrington. The thought twisted his chest, but he gave her his cockiest smile and tossed the dish towel onto the counter. "My first-floor elevation's already done."

With a chiding *tsk* and a shake of her head, she picked up the towel and hung it on the oven handle, adjusting the corners twice until they matched perfectly. "And I'm sure it's just as neat as you are."

Without another word, she tapped the light switch and left him standing in the moonlit room. "G'night, Colin."

"See you tomorrow, Gracie."

He heard a wooden board squeak as she ascended the stairs. "Don't count on it," she responded softly. "I'll be long gone before you're even awake."

That was making the assumption he'd sleep at all.

Who did he make happy? A woman to whom he owed his very life, or one who would never love him?

He couldn't win this one, no matter what happened. So he just yanked the corner of the towel and left it at a satisfyingly messy angle.

Mr. Harrington has requested daily faxes of your designs and a full report of any information on the competition's progress.

Gracie used the telephone message, written in Leonard's flawless script, as a coaster for her coffee cup. Not that the coffee stayed in the cup long enough to risk a spill. She'd devoured her third cup in an hour and still wasn't awake.

And it was nine o'clock in the morning.

There'd definitely been caffeine in that damn Earl Grey tea. So instead of sleeping off the midnight stroll and Black Forest cake, Grace had returned to a messy bed only to make it worse with hours of restlessness, punctuated by moments of bone-melting memories of one amazing kiss on the cliffs.

And just when she thought it couldn't get any worse, she'd stumbled into the studio to find that her father had called around the time she'd finally fallen asleep.

Checking up on her already. Early Sunday morning. He could have left a voice mail on her cell phone, but no. Much easier to shoot instructions at the help.

The message didn't say she had to call back, but she wanted to. Wanted to connect with him, with something familiar. Even if it was the chilly tones of Eugene Harrington. She felt terribly isolated in this temporary home.

Then she remembered it was *Sunday.*

Had Leonard told him she was still asleep? Would her father somehow be disappointed in that?

She popped her cell phone off the charger and dialed the number. After the second ring, Grace smiled when she heard the flat south-shore accent of Hannah Dumont. At least she didn't have to deal with her mother.

"Hello, Miss Hannah."

The older woman laughed heartily, as she always did when Grace used her childhood name for the housekeeper. "Hey, pretty girl. I just found out you're back in Rhode Island for a few weeks."

Hannah always knew where she was, and always made a point of letting her know it. It was as though the woman thought one of her many duties in running the Harrington house was to be the caring older woman in Grace's life…since Mother was rarely around to rise to the occasion.

"I am, Hannah. In Newport. How are you?"

"We're fine, dear. Your mother left yesterday for Vancouver, but your father's here."

"Vancouver? Didn't she just get back from the whose-a-macallits down in Virginia?"

Hannah laughed. "The Murray-Smiths, yes. But she's been invited to a friend's daughter's wedding and she's off again for the week."

"Well, that's Mother," Grace said with a sigh. "The perennial houseguest."

"Miss Catherine has a lot of friends and she does like to travel."

That was an understatement. Even though her parents' marriage had lost whatever glimmer of happiness it had ever had decades ago, it would be most unseemly for a Harrington to divorce. So Mother's solution was to travel as often and as far as possible, while Dad stayed home and ran the business. In both cases, they'd found lives that were centered anywhere but home. Which left one little girl alone quite a bit.

"Is he busy?" There was only one possibility for "he" in the Harrington house.

"He's in his office, of course. Hold on a moment."

While she waited, a movement outside caught Grace's attention and she looked down at the driveway, just in time to see the back of Colin's dark blue Porsche pulling onto Bellevue Avenue. Where was he going at this hour on a Sunday? Somehow she doubted it was church. Breakfast with his *friend?*

"Grace!" Eugene Harrington's booming voice vibrated the phone in her hand. "What have you got to report?"

She hadn't expected a term of endearment, but the thud of disappointment was there just the same. Or was that just residual displeasure from Colin's unexpected disappearance?

"Well, I only arrived yesterday, so—"

"Don't let that McGrath get a head start on you, Grace. I don't know what he's cooking up, but Gilmore likes it. He likes it a lot. But that's all I got out of him."

For a moment, she considered revealing exactly what McGrath was "cooking up," but something stopped her. "I'm not overly concerned about his ideas." That much was true. She wasn't worried about his ideas. It was his face, body, hair and, oh, yes, *his mouth* that had kept her awake all night. "I think Adrian was impressed with our designs and he particularly liked our approach of replicating the original masterpieces in the mansion as opposed to replacing them with similar items."

Her father made a grunting sound, as if he was drinking his own coffee. "But he wasn't impressed enough to hand us the project, Grace. He told me he wanted the overall design softened. I still don't have a blasted idea what that means. Have you talked to this McGrath fellow about his plans?"

Only when she wasn't kissing him out on Cliff Walk.

She cringed at the idea of blurting out the truth, even though screaming it in the back of her head was a game she'd played with herself since she could remember her first pressure-filled conversation with her father. She longed to tell him exactly what she was thinking. Of course, she didn't dare.

"Not very much. I doubt we'll see much of each other on this assignment. He—he keeps to himself."

"You should use this opportunity, Grace. Get to know him. And get over to the properties that Gilmore mentioned."

"I am," she assured him. "I'm touring the Breakers and Rosecliff today."

"Good. Then sketch out some improved designs immediately, and e-mail me your ideas. We'll work them over at the office."

"Of course." God forbid he just use her ideas, unchanged.

"You know Jack Browder is chomping at the bit to replace you out there."

Ah, the bait. Her father couldn't resist a stern warning about the dire consequences of not being a good girl. She knew all about Jack Browder's campaign to be chief architect on the Edgewater project. "I've heard," she said pointedly. "He's made his desires quite clear."

"There's some merit to the idea, Grace. Perhaps a man could develop a rapport with McGrath. Get to know what he's trying to sell Gilmore."

How many ways could her father find to let her know he

was disappointed she'd been born with the dreaded double-X chromosomes?

"Col—McGrath is not very communicative," Grace murmured, her gaze locked on the driveway as if she could will his car back. "I doubt even charming Jack could squeeze anything out of him."

"I'm golfing with Browder in an hour. We'll discuss it. Meanwhile, you keep working every angle. I want this job, Grace."

"Yes, sir. As do I."

There was no reason to say anything else.

Grace blew out a breath as she snapped her phone into the charger. *Love you, too, Daddy.*

She turned to the blank screen on her CAD system, but all she could see was the back of that sports car. Where was he going?

And why did she care?

With one click, she turned off the computer and decided to catch the morning tour of the Breakers, before Jack Browder bogied and eagled his way right into her assignment.

As she walked down the hall to her room, she noticed that the door to Colin's room stood slightly ajar. She slowed her step as she passed, absolutely unable to resist the urge to peek in.

All she could see from the hall was the disheveled, unmade bed and the sweatshirt he'd been wearing the night before, abandoned inside-out on the floor.

She wanted to focus on his sloppy lifestyle, but for some reason, her gaze traveled back to the rumpled sheets, and the imprint left by his head on the pillow. What would it feel like to wake up next to him one more time?

Would he be aroused, as he'd been last night when they kissed? Would he be gentle and tender? Or rough and fast?

That twisty, tingly, melty feeling started again and she forced herself to continue down the hall.

She had a job to do. Hadn't her father made that clear?
She'd be damned if that bonehead Browder was going to replace her and develop a "rapport" with Colin McGrath.

If anyone was going to develop a *rapport* with him, she was.

Gracie Harrington did everything with systematic precision. If she mentioned the mansion tours in a certain order,
Colin felt damn near certain that she'd written it down that
way in a planning diary and would visit them in exactly that
order. The Breakers, Rosecliff and the Elms.

He really didn't like the Breakers, with its absurd Renaissance opulence and hordes of gaping tourists. Rosecliff was
a much better place to meet up with Gracie.

The sprawling mansion sat far off Bellevue Avenue with a
commanding view of the ocean from the back. Colin took up
a spot in the front, near the vast fountain and pool, giving him
a wide-open view of the acreage and the tour groups as they
arrived.

While he waited, he forced himself to study the square lines
of the miniature version of Louis XIV's Trianon palace,
squinting at the gleaming white bricks and precise rows of
windows against the deep-blue September sky. His architect's
eye observed the classic exterior details, including paired
Ionic columns and arched French doors.

Everything about it was refined, classic and elegant.

Which, of course, was a perfect description of…Gracie.

Then his thoughts were right back where he didn't want
them. Gracie coming undone under the pressure of his kiss.
Gracie moaning with pleasure as his tongue teased hers.
Gracie admitting that her career hinged on the success of the
Edgewater business.

Oh, man. There was that circular thinking that had kept him
awake all night.

At least his sleeplessness had resulted in a plan. It would

take some doing, but if he succeeded, Gracie would get what she wanted…and so would he.

The trick was making Gracie fall in love…but not with him. That was categorically impossible—even if he believed there was such a thing as love, which he didn't. But if he could make Gracie fall in love with a different vision for Edgewater, then they'd both win. That was his goal.

As goals went, it was doable. Far more manageable than his fleeting, momentary hope of being her first lover. Not that he didn't ache for the privilege—*ache* being the most accurate of descriptions. But not with a girl who equated sex with love. No way. Sex was sex. Love was…stupid.

For a moment he thought of his brother, Quinn, recently engaged and ready to change his life. Maybe Quinn had forgotten what happened when you loved someone. Good for him. But Colin hadn't. And all indications from his oldest sibling, Cameron, showed that he had no intention of taking the chance on that kind of misery, either.

Nope. Sex and love were mutually exclusive. And as long as Gracie was looking for one with the other, he was not her man. Love was for doormats and dreamers. He'd learned that before he could read or write.

At that moment, he saw her enter the main gate with a small group of tourists and that familiar tightness took hold of his body. With her blond hair tucked under a Red Sox cap and a nondescript white sweater over khaki pants, she looked like a million other tourists—but he knew differently.

She couldn't completely hide her subtle, feminine curves. As she walked, he could see her breasts, small, but high and round, move with each step.

He took a steadying breath and watched her in animated conversation with someone in the ticket booth, practically able to hear the music of her laughter across the lawn.

He could live with the involuntary pull at the center of his masculinity. He was, after all, a man. But it was the other ache—the one in his heart—that had kept him awake all night.

As her group of about fifteen was shuttled toward the main entrance, he stayed behind the statue in the fountain. When she entered the building, he dashed to the ticket booth, paid and easily tagged on to the end of Gracie's tour.

In a few moments, after a young guide had droned on about the original owners of Rosecliff, they entered the ballroom. The speaker launched into the story of how *The Great Gatsby* had been filmed in the room, and the tourists looked around in wonder, as though they might find some evidence of Mia Farrow or Robert Redford in the air.

Quietly he stole up behind Gracie, her attention focused on the massive trompe l'oeil ceiling of painted clouds. He leaned close to her cheek. "Surely you're not thinking of *that* for Edgewater."

She jumped at the first word, but then closed her eyes and he couldn't read her expression. What was she hiding? Happiness? Or disgust?

"Actually, I was considering it for my bathroom in Boston."

He laughed, still close enough to get a whiff of her light, feminine fragrance. "It's girly, I'll give you that."

She finally looked at him from under the brim of her cap. "What are you doing here?"

"Following you." He grinned and laid a gentle hand on her arm. "I know this place better than the college-girl guide, believe me. Let's take our own tour and I'll give you the architect's viewpoint."

"How do you know Rosecliff?"

"I did a paper on the design for my Psychology of Habitation final." The crowd began to move out of the ballroom, but Colin kept his light grip on her. "I got an A."

He guided her in the opposite direction of the tour, taking her toward the famous heart-shaped staircase of the entrance hall. "Actually, I don't hate this mansion," he said as they reached the white marble floor of the entryway.

"That's damning with faint praise." Gracie laughed as she held a hand out toward the reception salon. "Really, Colin, what's not to like? Just look at that chimney piece."

They walked into the massive room, dominated by a hand-carved piece of Caen stone that filled nearly one wall. Ten-foot-tall crystal chandeliers sent a shimmer of soft light over the peach silk-covered walls.

"It's a little overbearing, but I like it," he admitted. "The owner had good taste. However—" he shrugged and indicated a sweep of the room with one hand "—there's nothing risky in here. It's all been done a million times since the seventeenth century."

She smiled at him, tipping the hat back a little and giving him his first good look at her face that day. She wore no makeup, but her green eyes were more naturally alluring than any colored eye shadow, even with the hints of darkness under them. So…she hadn't slept well, either.

"Considering it was a habitational psych class that got you to appreciate this building," she said, a smile lifting her lips just enough to draw all his attention to her pretty mouth, "you shouldn't be surprised. The designer created a room that reflected the mindset of the owner."

The urge to kiss her again was suddenly as fundamental as his need to breathe. "I agree with that. These people basically redefined the concept of self-absorption."

"What would you do differently, Mr. Avant-Garde Risk Taker?"

He glanced around the grandeur. "Nothing."

"Nothing? What, no glassed-in first story with a concrete floor to represent the urban carpet? Nothing?"

"Nothing…" He grinned at her, the room forgotten. "Nothing makes me as happy as you knowing my work."

Her cheeks flushed at the comment. "It's my business to know what the competition is up to."

"Good." The decision to take her to Willow House hit him like a hammer to the head. It was time. He took her hand and started toward the main hallway. "Then let's go."

"Why? I haven't finished the tour."

"You don't need to see this place, Gracie," he said, walking her briskly toward the front of the mansion. "If you want to find out what turns the competition on, then it's time to introduce you to someone very special to me."

As they took a few steps into the sunshine, she looked up at him with a teasing smile. "Is this the friend you had dinner with last night?"

"Yep. I hope you love her as much as I do."

Her smile disappeared instantly.

Six

Colin kept the top down on his car, making conversation nearly impossible. Which suited Grace just fine. Taking off her hat before the wind did, she'd corralled her hair with one hand and kept her focus on the yellow and black clapboard houses, the deepening reds and golds of the trees, and the pedestrians who peppered the streets. Anything but the girl she was about to meet.

No wonder he'd stopped that kiss on Cliff Walk. He was already in love with someone. A local. That was probably why he wanted the job so badly. So he could see his girlfriend on a regular basis.

She'd thought about arguing and refusing to go, but that would just seem small and petty. She was "developing a rapport" as her father had suggested. Surely Jack Browder would have no compunction about meeting the enemy's girlfriend.

She clung to that thought for the rest of the trip. Just beyond the Newport Hospital, he parked the car on a side street, in front of a stately, elegant red-brick house.

So the local girl had money, or she still lived with her parents. The home stood elevated on a hill, surrounded by a few lush acres of lawn and dotted with at least ten graceful weeping willow trees.

"This is Willow House," he said as he opened her door and held out his hand to her.

She climbed out and took in the expansive structure. "And this is where…your friend lives?"

"For the moment," he said with a wistful smile. "I'm afraid she won't be here too much longer."

She frowned a little and looked over his shoulder at the house. "Why not?"

"Because it's God's waiting room and my grandmother's about to be called in."

"Your…" She shook her head, trying to fit this fact into place. "You've mentioned your grandmother. Didn't you say she raised you and your brothers?"

He took her hand and started toward the house. "That's Gram McGrath. She's my father's mother. Marguerite Deveraux is my mother's mother." His voice was tight, uncharacteristically strained.

A strange, foreboding sensation settled over Grace with each footfall of her sneakers on the long asphalt driveway. She put her hand on his arm. "Where's your mother, Colin?"

She saw his Adam's apple move when he swallowed. "I have no idea. I haven't seen her since she left our house when I was three years old."

The revelation actually stopped her cold, but he opened the door and, with a firm hand on her lower back, urged her into a large front hallway. On the inside, the home looked nothing like the traditional colonial it was on the outside.

A long, hospital-like receiving desk took up most of the entry, with several chairs off to one side and a worn sofa on the other. Gracie was vaguely aware of a child on the sofa, but the woman at the desk laid down a novel and greeted them with a smile so bright, it blocked out everything else.

"Colin!" She reached out both hands over the desk. "Marguerite will be so happy you're back. When I combed her hair this morning, she just couldn't stop talking about how much she enjoyed last evening."

He took both of the hands offered to him, reached over the desk and kissed the woman's cheek. "If she's beaming it's because you're so good to her, Vera." He introduced Grace and then asked, "Do you think we could spend a few minutes with my grandmother this morning? Is she up?"

Vera held up one finger. "Just let me check on her, Colin. Last time I looked, she was resting."

"I'll tell her!"

Grace turned at the young voice, so loud and exuberant and out of place in the quiet home. A little boy not more than eight years old leaped off the sofa, letting a yellow plastic truck clatter to the ground as he did. "I know which one she is! I can check on her!"

"Wait just a second, bud." Colin reached out and snagged the boy with one hand, playfully holding him by the shirt. "Who are you here visiting today?"

"My great-granny Jane." He looked up with a serious face. "But she fell asleep right in the middle of a sentence. They do that you know. Anyway, my mom told me to sit out here."

Colin ruffled his dark curls. "Then you better do what your mom wants and we'll let Mrs. Sheppard do the honors."

The boy rolled his eyes a little. "If she's anything like mine, she's asleep anyway," he mumbled as he retrieved the truck.

Vera was back in less than a minute. "You're in luck, Colin. She's awake. I told her you were bringing your girlfriend in." She smiled at Grace. "That brightened her up quite a bit."

Grace opened her mouth to correct the woman, but Colin

grabbed her hand and didn't give her a chance. "Come on, Gracie. This way."

As soon as they rounded the corner, the house felt like a home again, with carpeted floors, soft lighting and soothing artwork on the walls. Only a long metal handrail lining the walls gave away the special needs of the residents.

At the very end, they came to a closed door with a brass number seven on it. Colin glanced at Grace, a warm look in his eyes. "Her vision is shot, but she can hear just about everything." With that warning, he tapped on the door and opened it slowly. "Marguerite? It's me."

The drapes were almost drawn, and a single lamp burned on the nightstand. A petite woman, so small that she looked lost in the double bed, rested in a half-propped-up position. The pillows under her head were laden with embroidered lace that matched layers of eyelet that covered the rest of the bed and the window.

The woman turned her head toward the door, moving a few wisps of thin, white hair. Even in the shadow, Grace could see her deeply lined face transform into a smile.

"Colin." Her voice was as tiny as she was. "What a wonderful surprise."

In one spare movement, he was around to the other side of the bed, taking a seat on the edge. "Hey, lady," he said softly as he leaned forward and kissed the top of her cobwebby hair. "I want you to meet someone."

She bent her elbows and tried to push herself higher on the pillow. "Where is she, honey?"

"Oh, please don't trouble yourself," Grace said as she approached a chair next to the bed. "I'll sit right here."

"This is Grace Harrington," Colin said. "Grace is an architect, Marguerite. She's working with me on Pineapple House."

With a start, Grace looked over the bed at him. She was? The old woman's smile widened even more, and she reached for Grace's hands with her own bony, spotted ones. Her fingers were warm and dry and so, so smooth.

"I'm sure Colin told you you're making a dying woman's dream come true. Thank you, dear. Thank you."

"You're not dying," Colin interjected, sounding like a father chiding an overly dramatic child.

"Yes, I am," Marguerite said as she squinted at Grace. "Come closer, dear. Let me look at you."

Grace leaned forward and the withered hand came up to her face. The woman laid her cool palm on Grace's cheek, the delicate fragrance of baby powder accompanying the touch. She caressed Grace's whole face slowly, her eyes closed as she examined. "Oh, my, what good bones. You're a pretty one."

Smiling, Grace put her hand on top of Marguerite's. "Thank you. So are you."

The woman grinned, showing yellowed teeth. "And do you like my Colin?"

"Most of the time," Grace answered with a soft laugh, looking over the slender body to the other side of the bed. His dark eyes were warm with humor and hope. He didn't have to worry. She'd never say anything to upset his little old grandmother.

"That's good," Marguerite said. "What do you think of Pineapple House, dear?"

Grace bit her lip and kept her focus on the crinkled face and dull brown eyes that stared at her. Those were Colin's eyes, she realized. Older, weaker and dimmed with age. But the resemblance was powerful. "It's—it's an interesting idea."

"Oh, dear child, it's more than interesting." Marguerite took a deep, labored breath. "Have you seen those wonderful sketches? They are—" She coughed, closing her eyes.

"Would you like a glass of water?" Grace asked.

Marguerite shook her head. "I'm fine." Then she patted her powder-soft hand over Grace's. "I only wish I'd last long enough to see it rebuilt. I'm the only living member of the Restoration Rebels. I'd like to greet the whole bunch up in heaven with good news about our pet property."

The Restoration Rebels? Grace was at a complete loss, and shot Colin a beseeching look. "I haven't heard about the, uh, Restoration Rebels."

Marguerite sighed and gave into another shaky smile. "Just a bunch of pushy, poor broads who liked to make waves." Her grip tightened slightly on Grace's hand. "The old Preservation Society bags hated every one of us, but we never cared. We made more noise with less money."

The woman turned toward Colin, who'd been very quiet during this exchange. "I'm so proud of what you're doing for me, dear. I know I've bored you with the story for years, ever since you found me."

Ever since he *found* her?

Marguerite reached out to pat Colin's hand. "You are one determined young man, I'll tell you that."

Colin held the woman's hand to his lips and kissed it. For some reason, the gesture seized Grace's heart in a vicelike squeeze.

"I'm just determined to keep my promises and pay my debts," he said.

"You don't owe me a debt, dear." She took another painful breath, and smiled weakly. "But I've no doubt you'll do this for me. And then you can bury me there."

"Stop it," he said softly. "You can bury me there."

She *harrumphed,* but it degenerated into a choking spell.

"I'll get her water," Grace offered, dashing into the adjacent bathroom. When she came back with a half glass of water, Marguerite's eyes were closed and a surprising little wave of panic washed over her. "Is she okay?"

Colin stood and pulled the blanket higher under his grandmother's chin, his hands looking gigantic against the diminutive woman. "She just fell asleep in the middle of a sentence." He grinned at Grace. "They do that you know."

She set the glass on the table next to the bed and gazed at the sleeping woman. "She's very sweet."

"She's very old. Almost ninety-three. I doubt if she'll make it to see Pineapple House built."

At the mention, Grace narrowed her eyes at him. "The project we're working on *together*."

He winked at her. "Thanks for not contradicting her."

"But it's not true."

He didn't respond, but leaned over the woman and kissed her gently on the forehead. Grace's poor battered heart nearly stopped at the tender gesture. He touched Marguerite's face and retucked the blanket under her chin.

She watched him reach down and turn off the lamp. Who would ever think that motorcycle-riding, earring-wearing, rebel-loving Colin McGrath would be so nurturing to a little old grandmother? A Restoration Rebel. Well. Some genes just carry on, don't they?

And then, the very heart that she'd been darn near ready to hand over to him stopped twisting and plummeted straight into her stomach with a sickening thud. If she won the Edgewater business, this dear old lady's dying wish would never come true.

Was that why Colin had arranged this tender little meeting with "the woman he loved"?

Grace suddenly realized she might have preferred a sexy young girlfriend to the sweet, sick old lady.

"It's blackmail, Colin. That's against the law."

Of course she'd think that. Colin gunned the Porsche into a sharp turn on Ocean Drive, the open ocean views blocked by the occasional contemporary showplace home.

"There's no law against visiting an old woman," he volleyed with a smile. "Anyway, she thinks you're my girlfriend."

"Another lie." Grace turned away from him as much as she could, and Colin blessed the tiny space of the Boxster. She couldn't get far. "Where are we going? This isn't the way back to Rosecliff."

"I love Ocean Drive." And that was true. But it wasn't why they were cruising the picturesque highway. If he'd taken her back to her car at Rosecliff, she would have disappeared for the rest of the day. He wanted a chance to talk, to plant the seeds of his master plan.

He pulled off the road to a spot that featured a breathtaking and unobstructed view, and killed the engine.

"What are you doing?" she asked.

He took a deep breath and gazed over the vast panorama of rocks and ocean and sky. "Just sightseeing. I think of Ocean Drive as New England's version of the California coast."

She didn't seem to notice nature's extraordinary artwork, but settled her accusing stare on him. "Why don't you start with a little background on the Restoration Rebels?"

Safe enough. And a good way to ease her into his plan. "The Restoration Rebels were a pretty colorful group of women in Newport. They were middle class, at best, and formed in the midforties and stayed together until most of them passed on."

He paused for a moment, remembering the funeral of his grandmother's last best friend. Marguerite, he knew, would join her soon. "They had this cause to stop the systematic destruction of the old colonial elements of this town, which were never quite as revered as the world-famous mansions. The mansions attract tourists and fill the town coffers. Even though they weren't wealthy, several of the Rebels had lineage back to the early 1700s."

"Did Marguerite?"

"No, but she loved a cause." He smiled, thinking of some of the talks they'd had. "And an underdog."

"Were they successful?"

"Somewhat, but not as influential as the all-powerful Preservation Society ladies."

"Where do Edgewater and Pineapple House fit into this?"

"When lightning struck Edgewater and burned down that mansion, Marguerite was thrilled. She was certain it was an act of some very rebellious angels. I would never have gone after a job like Edgewater; I turned down repeated invitations from Adrian Gilmore to bid on the job.

"But, about a week before the presentations, I came up here to visit her and she had these amazing sketches and managed to get me really excited about it. When I called Adrian to join the bidding, he just laughed as if he'd expected it all along. And, funnily enough, it's become the most important thing I'm doing."

Gracie turned to him, her green eyes bright, one slender finger aimed at his face in warning. "Okay. I understand. But you have to understand this: I will not be manipulated, Colin McGrath. Even by pity for your very sweet grandmother. I hate manipulation. I live with it every day with my father and if I can just prove myself—with this assignment—I stand a chance to get out from underneath that control."

"I'm not trying to manipulate you. I thought you should know that I have a pretty strong motivation for winning this assignment, too." But if the plan he'd hatched last night actually worked, couldn't he be accused of manipulation, too?

With a long, slow sigh, Gracie closed her eyes and leaned into the headrest, the sun shining directly on her face. After a moment, she opened her eyes and looked sideways at him. "What did she mean, 'you found her'?"

Colin thought about the day, nearly five years ago, when he'd walked up to the tiny house way out on Old Beach Road and knocked on the door of an elderly woman named Marguerite Deveraux. And about how she'd cried when he'd introduced himself.

"My mother was never particularly close to her mother," he said. "Evidently they had a very contentious relationship. My mother ran away from home when she was pretty young, lived all over the east coast for several years, and finally appeared to settle down when she met my dad at a bar in Virginia Beach. He moved her to Pittsburgh, and they had three kids. He did everything he knew how to put an end to what must have been—what must *be*—a pretty strong tendency toward wanderlust and itchy feet."

Already he could feel Gracie's piercing, confused, curious gaze. He hated telling this story as much as people hated hearing it. "But she took off on us and we never saw her again." He rushed through the sentence and waved a hand of dismissal. "Anyway, that's ancient history. About five years ago, I wanted to see if any other relatives on my mother's side were still around and a quick search on the Internet got me to Marguerite. I looked her up and we hit it off. End of story."

"What made your mother leave her family?"

Colin squinted into the sun. Hadn't she heard him? *End of story.* "I don't know."

"You don't know? No one's ever told you? Your father? Your older brothers?"

"We don't talk about her." He tried to take the edge out of his voice, get back to indifference. "All I know is that she read some women's lib book and bam! Out the door she went, never to be heard from again."

"No." The reaction of sheer incredulity wasn't unusual. People just didn't believe a woman could do that. "There must be an explanation. Was your father…abusive?"

He'd heard that accusation before, too. But he knew James McGrath was a man incapable of physical, emotional or any other kind of violence. "My father is a really good guy. I don't know what kind of husband he was, because I was a baby. But I know that he's got a good heart and he did everything humanly possible to raise decent kids, gave us great educations and made sure we wore white collars to work. That's how he measured his success as a father, and, based on our degrees and jobs, he nailed it."

"Do your brothers know you've found Marguerite?"

He nodded. "I told them, and they've both visited her." He didn't dare speak for his brother's hang-ups; he'd spent enough time trying to deal with his own. "We each handle our situation differently. We each have our own issues with what happened."

"What are yours?"

He toyed with the gold hoop in his ear, staring beyond Gracie to the horizon. "I figure I must have been the proverbial straw on the poor camel's back."

"How so?"

"One time I overheard two moms talking in a mall. This lady with a bunch of kids said to her friend, 'I was fine till I had him. The third one puts you over the edge.'" Turning from her piercing gaze, he placed both hands on the steering wheel and looked through the windshield. "As you can imagine, it hit home."

She put a gentle hand on his forearm, her touch warmer than the sun that poured into the car. "You can't possibly blame yourself for her leaving."

He couldn't? He turned back to her. "Let's put it this way. Now that I've gotten to know Marguerite, and she's told me more about my mother, I have a lot less guilt." He took a deep breath and blew it out slowly. "She doesn't realize it, but Marguerite really helped me to understand some pretty serious stuff. I owe her. Period. And I'm going to pay her back."

Gracie crossed her arms and leaned into the passenger door, giving him a long, thoughtful look. "Which leaves us right back where we started this conversation. You're blackmailing me to back off."

"No, I'm not," he insisted. "Really, I'm not."

"Then why did you take me to meet her if not to get me to back out of the bidding and let you build Pineapple House?"

He reached his hand across the space and touched her chin with his thumb. "I'm not going to build Pineapple House."

She narrowed her eyes. "You're not?"

"Nope. You are."

Grace just stared at him, her mind racing for some plausible explanation for what he'd said. There was none. "I am?"

He grazed her jaw with his thumb, sending all sorts of utterly distracting vibrations through her.

"I wanted you to come to that conclusion on your own, but I have a tendency to say what I'm thinking."

"I am not building Pineapple House. It's not what Hazelwood and Harrington wants to do with this property. It's your wild idea—and your grandmother's."

"Gracie, just give yourself time to think about the possibility. I won't try to coerce you into doing something you don't want to do." His hand engulfed the side of her face, his fingertips stroking the tiny hairs at the nape of her neck, making them all leap to instant attention. If that wasn't coercion, what was it?

"Take me back to my car, Colin."

"Okay, but…" He turned the ignition on and jerked the gearshift into reverse. "You have to eat lunch first."

No. Not another intimate dining experience at Zelda's. She couldn't take it. She had work to do and it had nothing to do with him or Pineapple House. "I'm not hungry."

"But Lenny packed us a picnic lunch."

She whipped her head around to stare at him. "What do you mean? You planned for this whole thing to happen today?"

"A guy can hope." He flashed a quick smile. "Anyway, we only have one more stop."

"Rosecliff. That's the stop."

With a shrug, he pulled back onto Ocean Drive. "Suit yourself. But Lenny made chocolate mousse. It's in the cooler in my trunk."

Good heavens, Leonard was in on this? "Chocolate mousse is really blackmail," she said.

"Come on, Gracie." He nudged her gently with his shoulder. "Come to Hunter House with me."

She scooped up her hair as they picked up speed. "Ah, yes. Hunter House. The excellent example of mid-eighteenth century Georgian colonial."

He laughed and pointed a finger toward her. "You were such a great student, Gracie. I remember that about you in college."

"I never had a class with you." She'd made damn sure of that. "How would you know what kind of student I was?"

He reached over and patted her leg, making her tense under yet another relentless touch. "I tracked your progress."

He'd tracked her progress? A jolt of satisfaction kicked her in the stomach. "Why would you do that?"

He lifted his hand to shift gears. "I had to."

She wasn't sure she wanted to hear this. "I don't understand. Why would you have to?"

He just laughed and took a curve so fast she had to hold on to the door handle. They zipped around another hairpin turn, and Gracie's whole tangled insides flipped at the dizzying sensation.

He finally slowed down as they hit traffic and veered toward the old historic district.

"You didn't answer my question," she said, trying to ignore the fact that they were *not* on the way to Rosecliff. "Why did you track the progress of some insignificant underclassman when you were so busy being a hotshot grad student?"

He grinned at her and barreled into an alley, then slid between two cars into a parking space. "You know what I love most about Hunter House?"

She was not ready to abandon the current conversation. Not

for one minute. But if she insisted, she'd sound...needy. "No, what do you love about Hunter House, Colin?"

He came around and opened her door, then popped the trunk with his keychain. "Way in the back of the property, there's this very secluded spot behind a tall stone wall."

"I've never been there." But she had the distinct feeling she might be...in the very near future.

"There are lots of trees and grass and absolutely no one can see you from the house. No one. It's completely private."

Her whole body tightened. "Really? Sounds lovely."

He pulled a red-and-white cooler from the trunk, and then scooped up the afghan she'd been under the night before. When did he pack that?

"It is *lovely.*" He said the word as though it pained him to use it, but then he melted her with the sexiest, smokiest gaze she'd ever seen. "I think it's the perfect place to tell you about the debilitating crush I had on you in college."

Seven

They'd devoured the chunky chicken salad sandwiches, polished off a container of freshly cut fruit, and nearly finished Lenny's miniature pie crusts full of chocolate mousse. But Colin hadn't said a word about his crush.

While he talked about Hunter House and about different aspects of Newport's history, while they debated the subtle nuances of Georgian colonial style throughout Revolutionary times, Grace kept hearing one phrase over and over in her head. *…the debilitating crush I had on you in college.*

Debilitating?

He never mentioned his bizarre idea about her rebuilding Pineapple House, and she was content to let it remain up in the wind on Ocean Drive. Maybe he'd been kidding.

She wanted to get back to that crush thing.

Sated by Lenny's scrumptious food and relaxed by the easy conversation, she lay back on the afghan. Closing her eyes against the speckles of sunshine glimmering through the leaves of a towering maple tree, she wondered how long she'd have to wait for him to pick up that thread of conversation.

But he wasn't talking. At least not about his crush. He was still musing about…*architecture.* Imagine that.

She turned onto her side, propping her head on her arm and watched him. He looked as comfortable as she felt, his long legs stretched out in front of him, his powerful torso leaning back on sculpted, muscular arms. A completely unexpected wave of desire tumbled through her at the thought of wrapping herself in those arms. Around those legs.

"The concept of a widow's walk always gives me the willies," he said, chewing on a reed of grass, his gaze locked on the roofline of Hunter House.

Architecture again. She followed his view to the rooftop enclosure visible over the stone wall that surrounded them. "Someone had to watch for those sea captains to come home."

"But so often they didn't come home," he noted sadly.

"And there you have your dreary name for an otherwise perfect finishing touch on a home."

He turned and looked at her, a half smile adding an enticing little crinkle around his eyes. "You like?"

His question referred to the style of house, but for a fleeting moment, she wondered if he meant him. Yes, she liked. Too much.

"I want to see the inside," she said vaguely, aware that she could be answering either question. She wanted to see the inside of him. To understand what made this complex, rebellious man so gentle with his dying grandmother. To touch the scars left by his heartless mother. To see if he was as achingly attractive inside as he was on the outside.

"We can go in later. Not now." He reached over and tickled her cheek with the blade of grass. "Let's talk about CMU."

Finally. "You first."

With a quick laugh, he slid down next to her. Not that

close, but their bodies were parallel. He mirrored her position by propping his head on his hand. She felt body heat rolling off him in waves.

"I liked you," he said simply. "A lot. Does that surprise you?"

Surprise. Delight. Thrill. The idea did a lot of things to her. "I guess. A little."

"And you?"

She gave him a tentative smile. "I think I made my feelings pretty clear one night."

"But you weren't…in control of your faculties."

She laughed at the euphemism. "Don't they say the truth comes out when you're drunk?"

He didn't say anything, but just smiled at her, the warmth in his eyes as intoxicating as anything a person could drink.

"I remember the first time I ever saw you, Gracie."

Her heart tripped. "Me, too. In the architecture library."

"You were wearing a dark green top that made your eyes—" He shook his head and paused, searching for a word. "Just incredible. And light-colored jeans. Like you have on now."

She couldn't believe he remembered what she'd been wearing. Of course, he was an architect. A visual man. And she remembered every detail of his clothes, as well. From his rolled-up sleeves down to the brown suede hiking boots. The ubiquitous ponytail. The little gold earring. Even back then.

"You were over in the design section," he continued. "Reading a textbook, but I noticed you were on the same page for over an hour."

She laughed guiltily, the sweetness of his reminiscences as delicious as the chocolate mousse she could still taste. "I was a slow learner."

"I kept glancing over, finding excuses to cruise by the study carrels." He twirled the piece of grass on the blanket in front of him, his gaze still on her. "Finally, I caught your eye on one of my sixteen trips past you. And you smiled."

She remembered the moment as though it had happened that afternoon. She could practically inhale the musty, papery smell of the stacks and feel the sputter of excitement every time he'd walked by. The way he'd devoured her with one look.

"You smiled back," she reminded him.

He gave her that same look now, that same smile. In an instant, time evaporated. And her stomach took the identical thrill ride it had taken in a library in Pittsburgh ten years earlier.

"You know what I thought, Gracie?"

She shook her head, incapable of answering.

"I thought you were a goddess. Beautiful, ethereal, utterly unattainable."

Her arm wobbled, threatening to collapse its support of her head. "Oh." It was the best she could manage.

"Now be honest, Gracie." He leaned an inch closer and tipped her nose with the blade of grass. "What did *you* think?"

"That you were the sexiest guy I'd ever seen." She rolled onto her back and covered her mouth with both hands. "God. I can't believe I just told you that."

He was above her in one quick movement, close enough for their bodies to practically touch. She felt the heat of his legs, his chest, his breath so close to her mouth. "You did? You thought that?"

She closed her eyes to block him out, but laughed again. "I think I made that pretty obvious long before I, uh, got friendly the night of the races."

"I did see you a lot that year. Before we…before."

She silently blessed him for being obtuse. "I probably wasn't too sly about figuring out where you'd be and showing up there," she admitted. "I was only eighteen, Colin."

"So you did like me."

Now there was an understatement. She closed her eyes and relaxed into what felt like a pretty silly grin. "I liked you bad."

His laugh was low, throaty and close enough to her ear to

tickle. "I liked you bad, too." He nuzzled her neck, a tantalizing, warm, sexual gesture that made her want to melt into the grass. "I wanted to kiss you every time I saw you, Gracie. Every time for four years. Did you?"

Kiss? She wanted to climb on top of him and…and… "Yes."

"When you saw me in the Student Union?"

"Buying drafting paper," she responded. "Yes."

"When you saw me on the quad?"

"Playing Frisbee. Yes."

"When you saw me on my motorcycle on Forbes Avenue?"

She narrowed one questioning eye at him. "Who was she?"

He laughed again, his lips against her temple now. "I don't remember her name. But I sure remember the look on your face."

With one finger on his chin, she pushed him back. "You liked bad girls."

"Past tense," he whispered. "Now I like good girls." He surprised her with one soft kiss on her cheek. "I like them bad."

She couldn't help laughing at his play on words, but she somehow resisted the urge to wrap her arms around his neck and pull him closer. "I don't understand this, Colin. You could have had any girl at CMU."

"No, I couldn't. I couldn't have you."

He couldn't? "You never asked me out. You never showed any interest. Except that one night. And…that wasn't reality."

"It was real to me."

She stifled a little moan at the low, soulful way he said it.

"When I came around the dining room that night and saw you standing there…" He punctuated the statement with another slow shake of his head. "I couldn't believe it. Gracie Harrington. In a frat house. With a glass of something wicked in her hand and a look that matched in her eyes." He grinned at her. "I couldn't believe my good luck."

"I went on a bet." She bit her lip and smiled at him. "My

roommate dared me to go and talk to you. She was sick of me talking *about* you."

He frowned at her. "But why'd you drink so much?"

"To get up the nerve to talk to you."

"Ah, Gracie. Who are you kidding? You were way out of my league and you know it."

She backed away to get a good look at him. "Out of your league? You ran with a crowd who didn't know I existed."

He settled onto his arm again, leaving a slightly safer distance between them. "Honey, you come from a crowd who doesn't *want* to know I exist."

"I don't understand you, Colin. What do you mean?"

"You're blue blood and I'm blue collar." She heard the flat tone of resignation in his voice.

"I don't know if that's true or if it makes a bit of difference," she said slowly. "But it certainly isn't something that would have stopped me from saying yes if you had asked me out. If I could have mustered up a coherent response."

"But it is something that stopped me from asking you out."

She turned on her side again to face him. "Well, that was plain stupid, Colin McGrath. You should have taken me off that pedestal you put me on in the library and asked me out." She couldn't stop herself from being as honest as he'd been. "We could have avoided that whole mess the night of the Buggy Races. Who knows what could have happened?"

"Nothing would have happened."

Nothing? She instantly regretted her honest little speech. "You…don't know that."

"Yes, I do. I would have put a stop to the whole thing before the inevitable happened." He leaned over her again, smelling like the fresh air, and the mint iced tea that Lenny had mixed.

"The inevitable?"

"You would have ripped my heart out, Grace Harrington. Just ripped it right out from my chest."

She froze, momentarily stunned by the depth of the pain she saw in his milk-chocolate eyes. "What makes you so sure of that?"

"Because I wouldn't have been able to stop myself."

"From doing what?"

He stroked her cheek with the grass slowly, making her wait for his response. "From falling in love with you."

A little breath escaped her lips as she closed her eyes. When she opened them, he was still there, close enough to kiss, and dead serious. Without pausing to analyze it, she reached out and touched his cheek, then trailed a finger along his lower lip.

"What makes you think I could have stopped myself from the same thing?"

His eyes darkened and his lips parted. Grace's whole body tensed in anticipation of the kiss. Her fingers itched to tunnel into his tied-back hair, her tongue ready to taste his.

With a jerk, he rolled over and stood up in one sudden, heartbreaking move. "We really ought to get home now, Gracie."

She felt as if he'd yanked the blanket out from under her and left her lying in the dirt.

He did it *again.*

Colin disappeared late that afternoon, leaving word with Leonard that he'd be out all evening. This time, Grace really wasn't hungry, so she opted to spend time in the studio, working on her designs, but she did more thinking than drawing.

She still couldn't believe Colin had had feelings for her ten years ago that had rivaled her own for him. Why was he convinced she would have "ripped his heart out" and not the other way around? Shaking her head, she flipped through the original designs for the Edgewater rebuild, searching desperately for inspiration.

But a shiver of disgust snaked through her as she looked

at her original presentation with a critical eye. The ideas presented to Adrian Gilmore on behalf of H&H weren't hers. Oh, she'd been in the room when they'd been discussed, but they were her father's. And Jack Browder's. And sixteen other senior architects who worked by committee.

What would she do, if given free rein?

She knew what she would do with "free rein." She would take his gorgeous face in her hands and kiss him. She would tear that leather tie out and let his hair fall around his face and bury her hands in the jet-black locks. She would climb on top of the rock-hard body and offer her...

Free rein could be a dangerous thing.

Taking a deep breath, she flipped to a blank page in her sketch book and forced herself to imagine a new Edgewater. A better Edgewater. A softer Edgewater.

But all she could imagine was Colin McGrath without a shirt on.

What had happened to Miss Virginity Until Love Conquered All?

She'd morphed into Miss Nail the Competition. Allie was right. What was next on her downhill slide into depravity? A bottle of champagne to celebrate her change of heart?

She startled at the sound of someone clearing their throat and looked up to the door. "Oh! Leonard." She didn't know if relief or disappointment filled her at the sight of the butler standing in the doorway, holding a large envelope in one hand, a cup and saucer in the other.

"I'm so sorry to disturb you, Miss Harrington. May I come in?"

She nodded and spun her chair away from the drafting table. "Sure, please do."

"I brought you some tea."

She smiled in appreciation. "And I was just fantasizing about something a little stronger."

"I would be delighted to bring you anything, Miss. A glass of wine, perhaps? A mixed beverage?" Leonard approached her desk with a serious expression, but something was definitely making those blue eyes twinkle. Maybe he could help unlock the mystery of what Adrian Gilmore was looking for with the rebuild of Edgewater. At least it would get her mind off…champagne.

"The tea is perfect, Leonard, thank you." She stood up to take the cup and saucer from him, and then tilted her head toward an empty chair. "Why don't you stay for a few minutes? I haven't had a chance to shower you with praise for the Black Forest cake." She took a sip of tea as he sat. "And the chocolate mousse! You are amazing."

Adjusting the neat creases on his trousers, Leonard sat and gave her a look of humility and gratitude. "Thank you, Miss Harrington. I love working in the kitchen. I really function more as Mr. Gilmore's chef than his valet, although I try to fulfill every need."

"It's a wonder the man doesn't weigh three hundred pounds, with all that chocolate."

He laughed and crossed his arms, the envelope he had now tucked out of sight. "I limit him to weekend splurges only. He's a very disciplined man."

"No doubt that's how he became so successful at such a young age. He can't be forty years old yet."

Leonard shook his head. "No, he's not. But he will be in a year. I certainly hope he settles down then."

"The Burger Boy billionaire?" Grace grinned over her cup. "Don't count on it. I've heard he's quite the player."

"I'm afraid it's true," Leonard said with a conspiratorial smile. "But he does believe in true love, so there's hope for him."

At the statement, Grace stifled a sigh. "True love? Jeez. Is there such a beast, Leonard?"

Leonard's eyebrows rose slightly. "Don't give up on it,

Miss Harrington. I'm sure it will find you at the most unexpected time. Oh! I nearly forgot." He held the large white envelope out to her. "Mr. McGrath asked that I give this to you. And I do so along with my heartfelt apologies. He left it on my desk with a note, which I didn't see until just now. I hope it's not something you need for what you're working on now."

Grace took the envelope, stifling the curiosity that came with it. What could Colin have left for her? "I doubt it has anything to do with what I'm working on. As you know, our approach to this business is very different."

"Precisely why having you two here was so important to Mr. Gilmore," Leonard agreed. "He told me last summer that he expected the two of you to be the finalists, and for the decision to be a difficult one."

Last *summer?* Grace distinctly remembered Colin telling her he'd turned down Adrian's invitation to bid until the very last possible minute. Could Colin be right? Could the Burger Boy have orchestrated this "showdown" between them?

Before she could figure out a way to interrogate Leonard further, he stood and repeated his offer of a different drink.

"No, thank you, Leonard." She'd have to think of another way of finding out the maneuverings that went on to pull off this odd arrangement. "I'll just have the tea."

"Good night then, Miss. I'll be turning in shortly."

Grace glanced at her watch. Was it that late already? "Oh, it's past ten. I wonder when Colin will be coming back." She could have bitten her lip as soon as she said it.

"He's returned, Miss Harrington." There was that little twinkle again. Did Leonard fancy himself a matchmaker? "I heard his car pull into the drive. But he hasn't come into the house. He's probably walking the Edgewater property. I've noticed he likes to do that."

When he left, Grace tore open the envelope. A stack of white paper fluttered out, copies of very light hand drawings.

At the top of the first page, in a stylized handwriting were the words: Pineapple House, 1743. Architect: Unknown.

Below it, a black-and-white artist's rendering of the front elevation of a beautifully balanced, exquisitely designed colonial home, complete with the ever-present widow's walk along the dropped hip roof and, of course, a carved relief of a pineapple over the front door. The architect in her admired every line, the even, rectangular windows and the simple, elegant design. And the woman in her wondered...*why?* Why had he left these for her to peruse?

The detail on every one of the twelve pages was astounding. The sketches included renderings of the large central hall, a massive rosewood banister and handcrafted cabinetry in sixteen rooms. On the last page there were no drawings, just handwritten paragraphs in a stilted, turn-of-the-century script, bearing the title *Biography of a Lost Landmark.* Grace read it slowly.

Pineapple House had been built by a prosperous sea merchant, and in its short hundred-year history, had hosted such illustrious guests as a Revolutionary War general, a U.S. Senator, and the Governor of Rhode Island. The words documented the many births and deaths that had occurred in the house and gave excruciating detail about the exquisite art collection as well as a priceless set of Newport pewter, both lost when the house was ultimately destroyed.

How could someone have desecrated this incredible piece of American history?

That someone, she realized as she felt her face melt into an embarrassed cringe, was her great-great grandfather.

A snippet of an old literary expression played in her head. Something about "the sins of the father."

Grace stared at the drawings, leafing through the pages until her tea turned cold, then returned to her original question. Why had Colin given her these? To pique her interest in building Pineapple House instead of rebuilding Edgewater? To make her see what could be done with this land? To touch her architect's soul and…blackmail her, again?

It was time they had a talk. She wanted to know his motives. She wanted to tell him about Leonard's slip about the timing of this arrangement. And she wanted to…

Oh, there went her imagination again. *Admit it, Grace.* She wanted to kiss him. A lot more than she wanted to discuss motives and land deals. She just wanted one long, lazy, sensual lip-lock that could be the icing on their mutual ten-year-long crush. Was that breaking a rule?

Without taking too much time to consider the consequences, Grace left the studio and darted down the back stairs to the second-floor hallway. Her door was closed; Colin's was wide open. His bed was made and the sheets had been pulled back and tucked in neat corners—evidence of Leonard's nightly turn-down. One light burned on the desk, illuminating an empty room. He must still be outside.

She continued down the main stairs, pausing to scoop the trusty blanket from the sofa. She inhaled the scent of the wool, expecting a reminder of the afternoon's picnic, but it smelled freshly washed. Good ol' Lenny, again. Tossing it around her like a shawl, she opened the front door and peered out over the enormous lawn of Edgewater.

Where would he be?

To her left, a hint of cloud-misted moonlight lit the north corner of the lawn. The section Colin's desk overlooked. The original site of Pineapple House.

Her loafers made no sound on the grass. She followed the moonlight and her instincts. At the edge of the lawn, a grouping of ancient oak trees had survived both the man-made destruction of this property a hundred and twenty years ago and the one nature had inflicted a few months earlier. Slowly, she approached the shadows, her blood pumping so violently that she thought he might *hear* her pulse before she spoke.

She knew why she was there. Looking for him in the dark. She knew why. Would he?

She paused, listening. All was still. No breeze. No crickets. No Colin.

"Did you like the sketches?"

She bit back a breath at the sound of his voice. Following it, as her eyes adjusted, she found him sitting on the ground, leaning against the trunk of a tree. He looked up at her with a knowing expression. Had he *expected* her?

"Yes." She dropped to her knees next to him. "Pineapple House is beautiful, Colin."

He reached out to her, his hand grazing her cheek as he turned her face to his. "So are you, Gracie."

And then he kissed her.

"Gracie."

Colin murmured her name into their kiss, loving the sound—and the minty taste of tea—on his lips. In one easy movement, he slid his arms around her slender waist to guide her onto his lap without breaking their kiss.

Hadn't he just been thinking about this? Dreaming of holding her, of loving her? And here she was. His goddess, his fantasy.

He whispered her name again and she settled into him, her arms tight around his neck. After a moment, she dropped her head against his chest. Somehow that was even more intimate than the kiss itself. A gesture of pure trust.

"Remind me to share sketches with you more often, honey," he whispered into the silken strands of her hair. "I like your response."

She looked at him, a gleam in her eye. "You kissed me."

"You kissed back."

"I'm only human, Colin."

He closed his eyes and eased her into a safer spot on his lap. "Uh, me, too, as you are undoubtedly figuring out right now."

He heard her tiny, sexy intake of breath. Oh, this was dangerous. Unexpected, romantic and completely dangerous.

Wordlessly, she leaned into him for another kiss, this one eliciting a gentle moan from her throat as their tongues tangled. Good grief, he couldn't do this for very long. He had to fight to keep his hands from exploring her, had to resist the urge to guide her over him and let nature start the ancient, rhythmic movement of man against woman.

"Did you come out here to make out in the dark, Gracie?"

She didn't answer for a minute. *Had* she?

"Not exactly."

Not *exactly?* If she came on to him, kissed him, held him and pressed her precious breasts against his chest, he couldn't be expected to stop, could he?

Yes. He could be. She was a virgin. She had no idea what she was doing to him. He took a deep breath and slowly, agonizingly inched her onto the grass.

"Then what *exactly* did you want?" He said it softly, with a laugh, but he needed to know the truth. Because if she wanted…

No. No. *No.* She wanted love. She wanted forever. She wanted a commitment where there wasn't one to give.

"Why did you give me the sketches, Colin?"

"So you'd kiss me."

She laughed. "Seriously."

"I wanted you to see them." Feeling moderately more in control of his urges, he put his arm around her and nestled her into his side. "Aren't they amazing?"

"They are. You didn't tell me the history. And the detail! Where did you get them?"

"The last of Marguerite's Restoration Rebels passed away

about six months ago, and willed her the sketches. They'd been hidden in an attic for over a hundred years. Some artist created them as the plans for Edgewater were being drawn up." He paused, enjoying the warmth of her against him. "What have you been doing all evening, Gracie?"

"Drawing."

"Really?"

"No. Thinking instead of drawing."

He chuckled. "Been there a few times. What were you thinking about?"

"You."

The word washed over him. "Not very inspirational."

"You got that right. I didn't get a thing done. But—" she pulled back a little to look at him with a serious expression "—I did have the most interesting chat with Lenny."

"Yeah?"

She nodded. "You might be right about Adrian. Lenny said he mentioned us as the finalists last summer. Didn't you say you only sneaked in a week before the presentations were held?"

"Yes. But for months before, Adrian was relentless in his pursuit of McGrath, Inc., on this." He leaned his head back against the tree, remembering some of the early conversations. "I was flattered, but, until I talked to Marguerite about Pineapple House, I had zero intention of going after this business."

He felt her cuddle deeper into the blanket and he pulled her closer just for the pure pleasure of it.

"Did you know I'd be involved?" she asked.

He waited a beat before answering. "I assumed H&H would bid."

"Is that why you didn't want to participate?"

"That was one reason."

"You didn't want to see me?"

"Not really."

This time she was quiet for the better part of a minute and finally asked, "Why?

"I think we about covered my debilitating crush this afternoon."

"You don't still have one?" She sounded so unsure, so scared to hear the truth. And yet, the truth was all he could give her.

"Yes, I do."

She lifted her face toward him, then her delicate fingers touched his cheek, and he turned to look at her.

"Me, too," she whispered.

Without warning, she took his mouth in a soul-wrenching kiss, lifting herself right back onto his lap.

"Gracie." As he murmured her name, he kissed down her throat and lifted his fingers to the V-neck of her sweater, caressing her collarbone and the delicate skin below it.

His head spun with need. His body tightened, straining his jeans and testing his every ounce of control.

He tried to ease her off his lap, but she leaned backward, falling gently on the grass. Helpless, he went with her, giving into the thrill of unimpeded body contact. He bit back a curse. He wasn't a saint, for God's sake.

"You're killin' me, honey." He heard the near growl of his voice as his hand moved naturally to the hem of her sweater. And under it.

He touched her warm, satin skin. She closed her eyes and drew in a breath, her hips rising against him.

He clenched his jaw. She kissed it until he relaxed.

He stiffened his hips. She slid her leg around his.

He held his hand firmly on her waist. She arched her back to give him access to her breasts.

She couldn't possibly know what she was doing with each sexy move she made. *Could she?*

"I know you're a virgin, Gracie, but surely you've spent

enough time with men to know that we're really helpless, pathetic animals." He punctuated each word with a kiss against the sweet skin of her throat and jaw. "We're not gifted with a surplus of willpower in this situation."

She laughed and the movement tightened her stomach right over his erection. Oh *man.* He moaned and let his head drop into the rise of her chest. "You have no idea how much I want you, Gracie." He couldn't stop himself. He kissed the flesh and brushed his hand over the thin material of her bra, over the swollen peak of her breast. "I want you."

He heard her gasp in response, then a strangled sound caught in her throat.

"Oh, Colin, I'm so sorry." Her voice cracked as she wriggled out from under him and he quickly moved his hand. She lay down next to him, their hips finally separated, but the heat still palpable between them. "I really haven't spent much time in a situation like…like this. But I'm not stupid. I do know what I'm doing."

She started to sit up, brushing a leaf from her hair. "And I'll stop. It's wrong."

"No, it's not wrong, Gracie." There was nothing wrong about what their bodies were screaming to do. But that was his opinion. She was waiting for *love.* "But this isn't how you want to lose your virginity, honey. Out here on the grass. On a blanket. Under the stars."

She laughed softly. "No, not when you put it that way."

He reached out and touched her lips, swollen from his kisses. "Put it this way. I'm not the man you want to give it to, Gracie." That would be one lucky SOB who wasn't a certified commitment-phobe.

She didn't say anything, but stood, her legs obviously shaky. "Don't be so sure of that, Colin McGrath."

Then she pulled the blanket around her shoulders and hurried back into the house.

Eight

Grace was still trembling when she closed her bedroom door behind her. What was happening to her? Had she lost her mind? There was a name for girls who played with fire like that. Several names, as a matter of fact. And none flattering.

She made her way into the bathroom, debating between a bath or a shower or just an old-fashioned howl at the moon, when she caught sight of her image in the mirror.

Who *was* that woman?

Certainly not Grace Harrington.

Her lips were dark and full, her cheeks flushed, her pupils dilated to the point of nearly obliterating the green of her irises. Her hair was tangled and wild and…was that a leaf in it? Her fingers grazed the reddened flesh of her chin, remembering the sexy abrasion of his unshaved kisses. Of his desire.

I want you.

Her insides still pulled, an unfamiliar achy tug that felt like a burning, unsatisfied hunger at the deepest part of her. Her arms and legs were numb, her breasts bursting with the need for him to touch her again. And again. And *again*.

She hadn't meant to be a tease, hadn't intended to respond like that, but this need…

I want you.

She'd hear those three words in her head forever.

Those were definitely not the three words that were supposed to send her to a lover's bed.

But, really, Gracie… She stared at her aroused reflection, liking the sound of his playful nickname, even in her head. *What are you waiting for?*

Someone better than Colin? She could look long and hard before she'd ever find a man who'd resist what he'd just resisted. She'd judged him all wrong. The demon with long hair and an earring, the rebel with an attitude and a big bad motorcycle was…no rule-breaker.

He was a good man.

An image of him kissing his grandmother's aged hand flashed in her mind. Hadn't that one simple gesture demonstrated exactly what kind of man he was?

Maybe this wasn't love. Oh, there was no maybe. This *wasn't* love. This was *want*.

And tonight, *want* beat *love* all around.

Turning from the mirror, she walked to the dresser and yanked open the bottom drawer. Inside, her casual clothes were folded and organized by color and fabric. She lifted a shirt, flipping it to the floor and liking the freedom of that. She tossed the pink sweater that Allie had said she'd soar in next to it.

Then she found what she wanted to wear. What she'd worn a hundred times in the last ten years, always fantasizing about him touching the now-worn fabric, taking it off…

She stripped off her pants, sweater and bra, and stood fingering the unadorned edge of her functional white satin underwear. It wasn't "old lady" underwear, but it sure wasn't anything like the whispers of lace she'd seen piled in Allie's laundry basket. She didn't own such a thing.

So it would be nothing at all.

She stood naked in front of her dresser, refusing to give herself too much time to think about this. A chill skittered over her skin in the cool night air, reminding her that she'd left her window open. Unfolding the soft cotton, her fingers grazed the lettering, remembering the feel of it against her skin the first time she'd worn it.

She tugged the T-shirt over her head, and let it fall midthigh. Yes. This was what she wanted to do. She had no doubts. No second thoughts. And there would be no regrets.

I want you.

In fact, she'd never stopped wanting him.

And now it was time to pick up exactly where they'd left off.

The ice-cold shower helped. At least it eased the incapacitating physical response that had made it difficult for Colin to walk back into the house. Good Lord, who knew Grace Harrington could torture a man like some kind of wanton lap-dance queen? She had no freaking idea how sexy she was.

He twisted the cold-water spout and reached for the towel he'd left hanging over the shower door, giving his hair a quick swipe, and then wrapping the towel around his waist. He'd never sleep. If he did, he'd wake up...hard and unsatisfied.

How the hell was he supposed to live in this house for the better part of three more weeks? He picked up his toothpaste, used his brush to flick off the hard crust at the top and squeezed a clump on the bristles. What were his options?

Options? Oh, yeah. *They* were plentiful.

He outlined a list while he brushed. He could spend the

next three weeks taking hourly cold showers. He could convince her to abandon her values and morals for a quick, but desperately needed, roll in the proverbial hay. He could go find another woman and pretend it was Gracie.

The last one made his stomach lurch.

Nope, none of these options had the remotest chance of success. What could he do? He stared in the mirror, his brush frozen, toothpaste foaming around his lips.

He could love her. Marry her. Spend the rest of his life basking in the glow of Gracie.

He nearly choked, spitting hard in the sink.

Get real, McGrath. Even if he suddenly did a one-eighty and decided to take a chance on the unthinkable, she'd prove him right and run like hell the minute she saw the humble house he'd grown up in on Brownsville Road. They were from different stratospheres.

He picked up the tube of toothpaste and stared at it, crushed in the middle and speckled with dried paste. Of course, if his blue-collar background didn't scare her off, no doubt his personal habits would do the trick the first time she took a good look around his bathroom.

He began a cursory search for the lid, but abandoned it, dropping the toothpaste on the counter before heading to bed. In the bedroom, he flicked the towel off, let it fall at his feet, then snapped off the desk lamp. He considered closing the drapes against the moon that bathed the room in an eerie half light, but then he'd sleep late and he wanted to run in the morning.

Sleep? Right. As if he could sleep knowing she was across the hall. In her bed. Wearing nothing but—

He froze, the sheet suspended in air as he was about to get into bed.

Wearing nothing but his old CMU T-shirt and a smile.

He knew he was gawking, knew he was naked in front of her, but he was helpless to move. Time and space and atoms suspended around him. He couldn't think. Couldn't fathom what was happening.

A drop of shower water from his hair snaked down his back as he leaned just a little bit closer to be sure this wasn't your basic mirage.

Nope. It was real. Gracie was in his bed, tucked so far down into the covers he'd almost missed her.

"I think you took a wrong turn, honey," he finally said, sliding into the bed beside her before she saw the effects of a cold shower disappear, and the effects of *Gracie* return full force. "This is my room."

"I know where I am."

He turned on his side, not touching her, but not quite ready to kick her out, either. "You do?"

She nodded.

"Do you know what you're doing here?"

She nodded again, her eyes wide and glinting with a wicked spark.

Oh, man. She wanted love. She wanted love. *She wanted love.*

The mantra wasn't working. He just grew harder and then…he touched her sleeve.

"Nice jammies."

"I'm returning this to you."

He grinned. "It's about time."

"Of course, if you want it back," she said with a surprisingly provocative smile, "you'll have to take it off me."

His gut tightened. His throat closed. His brain shut down and another organ happily seized control. *Take it off her?*

Oh, *man.*

He took a long, deep breath, fighting every cell in his body that wanted to smother her with kisses and end this agony by pounding himself into her. Take it *off* her?

"You really don't know what you're doing, Gracie. You don't want to do this."

"Yes, I do." The look in her eyes was pure honesty. Deep forest-green and as hungry as he felt, yes, but she was telling the truth.

"You want love," he ground out. *Didn't she?* "You told me you were waiting for your first true love."

She reached over and lifted a strand of his hair, then twirled it around her finger. "I want you, Colin McGrath. I've been waiting for you."

Humor and control and good old-fashioned morals vaporized in the face of that declaration.

She wanted *him.* "Are you sure?"

"I've never been more certain of anything in my life."

She *thought* she was sure. But, tomorrow, how would she feel? Once she'd experienced this, would she still want him as much? What if that look of pure desire disappeared after she'd lost her virginity, only to be replaced by that icy protective shell she'd wrapped herself in last time they woke up together?

Could he take that risk?

Could he *not?*

"Are you sure, Gracie?" he forced himself to ask her again. "Are you absolutely, positively certain that you won't regret this and hate me in the morning?"

She let out a tiny, surprised laugh. "I thought I was supposed to be the one who worried about that."

"You never have to worry about that, Gracie. I could never hate you. I—I—" He *what?*

Before he could complete the thought, she slithered into his body, flattened her palms on the planes of his chest and pressed herself against the full length of him. His breath caught at the incredible sensation of her bare legs against his. Silky. Her legs were like long, tight ribbons of silk wrapping around him.

He ran his hands down her back, grazing the T-shirt—*his* shirt that she'd kept for *ten* years—until he reached...bare skin.

She had nothing on under it. Nothing. The flesh of her backside was so soft, so indescribably smooth, he moaned as he curled his fingers into her, loving the feel of satin skin over her tight muscles.

"I hope you know what you're doing, Miss Harrington." He guided her onto her back and balanced himself above her, supporting his weight by placing his arms on either side, trapping her under him. But she wasn't trapped. He'd given her every opportunity to change her mind. However, his superhuman restraint was damn near gone. "'Cause I am officially about to break some rules."

She just looked at him, that brash little grin back in place. "Good. I've had all the rules I need for one lifetime."

His mouth came down on hers with more force than he'd intended, but she sucked his tongue as her hips rose against him. She tasted like the spearmint of his toothpaste and smelled like flowery soap and lemon shampoo. And the sexy tang of female moisture.

At the thought, his erection jammed between her legs and a panicked breath escaped her.

"Don't worry, don't worry," he reassured her with a flutter of kisses, lifting himself a bit. He wiped her cheek where a drip of water from his hair drizzled, grateful it wasn't a tear. "I'm only losing control, not my mind. I know this is your first time." He *had* to find some measure of discipline and take this easy. He couldn't hurt her. Not after she'd trusted him.

"We'll go nice and slow," he promised. Kneeling over her, he fluttered the bottom of the T-shirt. "By the way, you look really cute in this."

"Thanks."

"Now let's get rid of it."

He raised the shirt, thanking God he hadn't closed the drapes. He wanted light. He wanted to drink in the sight of her. As he lifted the material, he saw a honey-blond triangle of hair and the most deliciously concave dip in her stomach. His jaw slackened at the sight, but he continued to undress her, drinking in the sexy curve of her hips and her tiny waist. Her body trembled under his gaze, and he looked up at her, noticing the wonder and doubt in her eyes.

And then it hit him. No one had ever *seen* her before, either. She was for his eyes only. He struggled with a ragged breath, as he exposed her beautiful breasts, small and round and, magically, as elegant as she was. He finally guided the shirt over her head, his mouth practically watering to taste and suckle her.

She took the T-shirt from his hand and threw it over his shoulder to the floor, eliciting a surprised laugh from him.

"Oh, no. I've created a monster," he said, kissing her eyelids, her cheeks, her lips and throat.

But she just arched into him and pushed his head lower. He took one dark-pink nipple into his mouth and began to suck gently, licking it to a hardened tip, then devouring it again. His hand covered her other breast, kneading the delicate flesh, grazing the peak with his palm. Her hips had developed a rhythm of their own, rising and falling, rocking and pushing against him, rubbing his shaft with each heart-stopping contact.

He took her hand and guided it between them. "Touch me, Gracie." As her fingers wrapped around him, he closed his eyes and groaned softly. She could barely encircle him and the thought made him instantly harder. And scared. Would he hurt her?

He would be so careful. He would. But now he quaked and stiffened in her hand, burying his face in her hair and covering her with hot, insistent kisses. Lovingly, effortlessly, she stroked him. He lifted his head and their gazes locked, a million tender, unspoken words passing between them.

Her hand curved around the tip of him, gliding over the slick surface. "I want you to be inside me, Colin."

The amazing honor of it struck him again, and he longed to promise her to be worthy of this.

Closing his eyes, he gently kissed her. "Thank you," he whispered into her mouth. "I'll take care of you."

He deepened the kiss, tracing her teeth with his tongue, sucking gently on her bottom lip. He touched her everywhere he could reach, letting his hands take a torturously slow journey over her skin, filling himself with the pleasure of feeling Gracie under him. He suckled her breasts again, holding each in one hand and nuzzling his face in her cleavage just to inhale the sweet fragrance of her sweat-dampened body. He licked her tummy, kissed her hipbones and paused to worship her navel.

With each caress, each kiss, her fingers buried deeper into his hair. Blood coursed through his body at a wild rate, singing and screaming so loudly he could barely hear her murmurs of appreciation and pleas for more.

Once again, he leaned above her, and carefully nudged her legs apart. Holding her gaze, he curled his fingers into the soft tuft between her legs.

She closed her eyes and sucked in an uneven breath, then relaxed to let him tease the slick folds of her skin. She quivered and squeezed against his finger, making the achy need to be inside her suddenly so primal and driving, he couldn't breathe.

But he had to take her at a pace she could handle. Not the one his body was demanding. He whispered her name, coaxing her along. "Do you like that, honey?"

She nodded, a helpless, faraway look on her face as he felt her body begin its complete surrender.

He slipped one finger inside her and she rocked into it, muttering a plea for more. He kissed her mouth, matching the strokes of his finger with his tongue. His shaft pulsed against her leg as he opened her wider and tenderly inserted two fingers.

She tightened as a tremor vibrated her swollen flesh. She turned her head to one side, then the other, breathing his name. He had her at the edge, ready to shatter. Ready for him.

"Gracie, are you sure you want me to be the first one?"

"Yes, yes, please." The subtle break in her voice nearly did him in. "Colin."

He eased his fingers out of her and embraced her tightly, fighting the sucker punch of emotion that ricocheted through him. "Promise me, Gracie," he whispered. "You won't hate me tomorrow."

She moaned a half laugh and shifted into him, enveloping his erection with her thighs. "I *promise,* Colin. No hate. No tomorrow. Just, *please.* Don't stop."

She arched her back, forcing the tip of his penis into her slick folds.

"Wait." He eased off her to open the drawer of the nightstand and she groaned in frustration, making him smile. "I was actually prepared for this," he said softly, grabbing a foil-wrapped condom he'd bought the day he'd moved to the carriage house. Before he knew he'd be her *first.*

"You were?"

"I didn't know—" He shook his head, unable to discuss anything coherently. "Later, honey. I'll tell you later. I'm gonna die if I don't make love to you."

Make love? Is that what they were doing?

It sure felt like it to him.

He rolled the clear sheath over his erection, then he levered himself on top of her. "I want this to be so amazing for you, Gracie," he said as his shaft found its natural home at her opening. "But you might—it might hurt."

"Shh. It's already amazing." She lifted herself again, and he inched into her. "It doesn't—" She bit her lip and looked at him, a flash of pain and surprise in her eyes as he felt her flesh stretch to accommodate him.

He started to back out. "Oh, Gracie, I'm sorry."

But she shook her head furiously, grabbing his buttocks and pushing him back inside her. "Don't stop. It's okay. I want all of you, Colin."

Her words—her honest pleas—were too much for him. A white light exploded in his head and he burrowed deeper into her, giving in to the clutch that controlled his body.

He heard her gasp and he tried to stop moving again, but she wrapped her legs around his hips and rocked against him until he was fully hilted, her hot, taut opening enveloping him.

Calling out at the intense shock of pleasure, he froze for a second, waiting for her reaction.

"Don't stop." She mouthed the words, apparently unable to find her voice, as she guided him in and out, refusing to allow a pause in their dance. With each gradually increasing stroke, her breathing steadied, her grasp relaxed and her expression transformed from surprise to arousal to mindless pleasure.

He and Gracie were finally connected.

The thought squeezed his heart. He drove into her with more confidence and abandon, letting their perfect synchronization increase in speed, as their slick, heated bodies entwined and their breathing grew rough and loud. They clung to each other, riding an unstoppable wave to the same place.

Sweat stung his eyes and he squeezed them closed, clenching his jaw as the pressure built up to something wildly close to pain. His lower back tingled and tightened, he was bursting with the need to explode.

Gracie's fingertips impaled his arms and her legs tightened in a vise grip around his hips.

Her flesh squeezed and spasmed around him, her eyes fluttered, and she sunk her teeth into her lower lip as she finally, blessedly lost all control. She slammed against him again and again and again, thundering with an orgasm, just as his own unrelenting need for release obliterated everything but the insane, impossible reality of losing himself inside Gracie.

Nine

A vague awareness of déjà vu floated over Grace before she was fully awake. She'd been in this place before. Involuntarily, she steeled herself against the inevitable fleeting terror, followed by the nauseating sense of self-loathing.

She opened her eyes, and squinted into the early rays of dawn. Without moving a muscle, her gaze slid to the floor and landed on the T-shirt, inside out, balled up next to the bed. The impulse to dive out of bed to right that wrong was stopped dead by the powerful arm locked around her stomach. And the hard, unyielding body that curled into her back.

Colin.

She closed her eyes again and waited. Terror. Self-loathing. Nausea. Directly ahead.

But there was…none.

No terror at all. On the contrary, she felt wrapped in a veritable envelope of safety. She didn't loathe anyone. In fact, a surging of goodwill for all mankind tingled in her chest. Nausea? The only thing going on in her tummy was…*oh.* That delicious achy, twisty, pulsing thing that happened every time she was in the same room as Colin McGrath.

Her first lover.

She closed her eyes and remembered the long marvelous night they'd shared. She thought of how he'd brought a warm, damp washcloth to the bed after they'd made love and held it between her legs. There'd only been a few streaks of blood, and the pain was minimal. But his caring had touched her beyond description.

And when he woke her in the middle of the night, his kisses had covered her body so thoroughly she thought she'd scream into the darkness, as he suckled her into an incredible vortex of another orgasm with his mouth and tongue and magical hands. Then they'd made love so slowly and so tenderly, she'd had to fight tears as he released himself inside her, repeating her name like some kind of prayer.

This wasn't the love she'd been holding out for, she reminded herself. But she hadn't sold out. She *hadn't.* It might not be love, but it was the most satisfying thing she'd ever experienced.

He stirred behind her, shifting his position. "Tell me something, Gracie." His lips seared her shoulder with a kiss. "What made you change your mind?"

She turned slowly in his arms, closing her eyes and adding a sleepy, throaty moan, prepared to feign slumber rather than answer questions that she…couldn't answer. He pulled her directly into his chest, surprising her with the steady—and rapid—beat of his heart. Not the thumping she'd felt against her when they made love. This was more like…*anxiety?* The possibility that anything, anything at all, could scare Colin filled her with the strangest sense of wonder.

She fluttered her eyes open. "Oh. Hi." She smiled, amazed again at how handsome he was, his morning stubble and sleepy eyes as sexy as his post-shower sleekness the night before. "Did you say something?"

His look told her he wasn't the least bit taken in by her act. "You heard me."

She mentally rummaged through a dozen possible responses, discarding each. What could she tell him? That a piece of her heart had broken off when he'd kissed his ailing grandmother's hand? That she'd just grown tired of clinging to some arbitrary rule she'd made up after she'd been hurt in college? That he'd simply sucked all common sense out of her brain and wakened a woman who'd been asleep for twenty-eight years?

No. The fact was she didn't understand her change of mind—or heart—any better than he did. And she didn't want to examine it too carefully. At least, not now. He quietly repeated the question. "What changed your mind?"

"Why is that important?"

He tunneled his fingers into her hair, lifting her face to his. "I want to know."

"It's not important."

"It is to me."

She walked two fingers up the phenomenal breadth of his chest, loving the tendrils of coarse black hair that curled over it. She practically shivered, remembering the rough feel of his completely masculine torso against her breasts, the sensation of his midnight beard against her thighs. And his demanding, enchanting tongue when it found her...

She sighed contentedly. "I'll tell you what's important."

"Hmm?"

"I liked it."

A slow smile lit his face, his eyes glinting. "I could tell."

"No, I *really* liked it." She lowered her voice to the faintest whisper. "I want to do it again."

He responded with an easy sway of his hips, a relentless erection stabbing her tummy. "That can be arranged."

"And again," she said.

This time he just raised his eyebrows.

"And a couple more times after that."

He started laughing.

"And then after dinner," she continued. "Before we go to bed again."

He laughed so hard the bed shook.

"You *have* created a monster," she announced, unable to keep the pride and victory out of her voice.

He managed to stop laughing and tried to look serious, but there was moisture and mirth in his eyes when he finally could talk. "I always knew I was the luckiest guy in the world." He shook his head in dismay. "I can't even believe my luck."

She pressed herself against the length of him. It was so much easier—and way more fun—to *do it* than talk about *why*. She snuggled into his neck, her gaze locked on the simple gold earring. She just wanted to…flick her tongue over it. She started to slide her hand over the rippled muscles of his back, reaching her mouth toward his earlobe.

"Uh-uh." He held up one finger to stop her. "You haven't answered my question."

The man was crazy. "I realize I'm no expert in the field, but don't guys generally prefer sex to conversation?"

"I'm not like other guys."

Wasn't *that* the truth? "Then you've answered your own question, Colin."

He gave her a perplexed look. "I don't follow."

"You're not like other guys." She tipped the earring with her finger, as the perfect punctuation to that statement. "That's what changed my mind."

"Really?" He gave her a dubious look. "And here I thought it was my remarkable architectural skills."

Laughing, she wrapped her legs around him and let him pull her on top of him. "Oh, those are wonderful, too," she said, easing her body over his so that his chest hair tickled her breasts. "I particularly like your horizontal structure compression member. It did a number on my expansion joint."

He rolled his eyes at her puns, then he blew out a breath that was half laugh, half amazement. "I can't believe this is happening."

"Believe it." She leaned over and yanked the nightstand drawer open. "How many did you buy?"

He grinned. "Evidently, not enough." He slid his hands over her backside and adjusted her to their perfect fit. "We'll send Lenny for more."

"No!" she gasped. "We will not."

He started laughing again. "Oh, it's okay to do it morning, noon and night, but don't let anyone know." He flipped her over on her back, seized her hips between his legs and encircled each of her wrists with a gentle, but firm grip. "I'm not ashamed of this."

"It's just…private," she insisted, trying to tug her hands free.

He skimmed his hands down the insides of her arms in one long sweep until he reached the sides of her breasts. "We can keep it private, Gracie." He rubbed the pads of his thumbs over her nipples, sending electrical impulses straight through her. "But he'll figure it out soon enough when we don't come out of this room for ten hours."

The reminder of Lenny brought much needed wisdom to her overloaded senses. "I'd better go to my own room."

"Don't even think about it, honey." Colin flicked his tongue over the budded tip of her breast. "He won't do a bed check."

"But he gets up early and makes me coffee."

He lifted his head and gave her a skeptical look. "Does he bring it to your room?"

"No, but if I don't show up for it, he might wonder." She didn't want to get caught. Not like this. Not yet. "Let me get a robe from my room, run down and get a couple of cups of coffee, then I'll be back. Then I can stay…under the covers for a while. How's that?"

She struggled to get up, but he pinned her with a long, demanding kiss. "Don't take too long," he murmured into her lips, deliberately sliding himself between her legs. "My I beam is lonely."

"Oh. That's bad. Very bad, Colin." She elbowed him away with a grin, climbing out of the bed and snatching the T-shirt. She tugged it over her head, without even turning it right-side-out, a move that elicited another heartfelt laugh from him. Blowing him a quick kiss, she slipped out the door.

In her room, she glanced at the bed that had been turned down by the butler, but not used by the guest. What would Leonard think?

He'd think she'd made her bed, of course. She quickly pulled the covers up and smoothed the pillow cases. Nothing odd about that. She was a certified neatnik. When she went to the bathroom to brush her teeth, she saw herself in the mirror.

Well, she *used* to be a certified neatnik. If he looked too closely at her, ol' Lenny would know that she'd *transformed* into someone else overnight.

Knotting the ties of her bathrobe, she tiptoed downstairs, smelling the rich aroma of Leonard's brew by the time she got to the living room. She wouldn't have to lie to the butler, if she saw him. He'd ask if she had a good night and it would certainly be the truth to say, yes, as a matter of fact she had. The best night of her life.

Fighting a sly smile as she turned the corner, she heard his smooth British accent from the back office, adjacent to the kitchen.

"Absolutely, sir. I'm watching for that very thing."

Was he talking to Adrian? Grace paused, biting her lip and listening for a second.

"Of course, Mr. Harrington. There'd be no doubt of that."

Mr. Harrington? Her father was on the phone? At six-fifteen in the morning? She stifled a groan. Checking on her progress, naturally. She took another step toward the coffee, but stopped at the sound of Leonard's voice, unable to resist eavesdropping on a conversation that involved her father.

"Oh, no, sir, not at all," he said seriously.

What had her dad asked? He probably wanted to know if she'd "developed a rapport" with the competition yet. Well, Lenny the answer is a resounding *yes.* An excellent rapport. Didn't he hear that rapport shaking the rafters of the carriage house last night? She stifled another little giggle, but caught herself when he started talking again.

"That's true, sir, but you cannot possibly control the outcome, as I warned you and Mr. Gilmore when we worked out the details of this arrangement a month ago."

This arrangement…a month ago?

Was her father behind this from the beginning?

Leonard chuckled softly, and Grace willed the blood to stop rushing in her ears so she could hear. "Not to worry, sir. I rise at dawn daily. You may continue to call and I'll inform you of any progress. That's been our plan from the beginning, and Mr. Gilmore is delighted to assist you."

All the terror, self-loathing and nausea she'd been expecting hit Grace with the force of a tsunami wave.

She laid her hand on her chest as though she could stop the hammering of her heart. It couldn't be. *It couldn't be.*

Her father had arranged this with Adrian Gilmore. The ice-cold shock of it made her start to shiver as she backed out of the kitchen slowly.

Why? Was she some kind of pawn in their weird game? Was he testing her? Were they trying to make it look like a legitimate bid, when H&H had the business all along?

She spun on her bare foot, ready to scamper up the stairs

and hide in her room. She couldn't face Leonard, she had to be alone to figure this out.

"Oh, Miss Grace, good morning to you." She stopped at the sound of his clipped greeting.

Slowly, she turned to face him. He looked chipper, his thinning hair slicked back, his butler's uniform of a white shirt and black pants as stiffly pressed as always. Normal. Smiling. "Good morning, Leonard."

If he noticed the chilliness in her voice, he ignored it. Instead, he opened the cabinet and pulled out a coffee mug. "Didn't you want any coffee this morning, ma'am?"

She stared at him. Wasn't he going to tell her who he'd been talking to? "Uh, yes. I would. Thank you." She took a deep breath. "I thought I heard you on the phone, so I was leaving to give you some privacy."

"Not necessary, ma'am. It was just Mr. Gilmore's office in London. It's midday across the pond and they've no concept of the time difference, I'm afraid."

Lenny was a liar. She felt her jaw begin to go slack in amazement, but she caught herself. Two could play this game. Now she *knew*. And knowledge was power.

"I hope everything is all right," she said casually, taking the cup he handed her.

"Oh, of course, ma'am. Business is booming at Burger Boy."

She gave him a faint smile and sipped. "That's good." How could she ask him for another cup? How would she explain bringing coffee to Colin?

Oh, God. How could she tell Colin of her horrible discovery?

The thought made her legs weak and sent her heart plummeting to her stomach. He would hate being used like this. She knew him well enough to know being a victim in a devious scheme would go against every fiber of his being.

But Colin had been right all along. Lenny was a spy. And the whole thing had been set up long ago. By her *father.*

"And you'll be heading up to the studio this morning, ma'am, so Mr. Colin can have his time in the afternoon?" he asked as he approached the sink and began sprinkling water on a row of fresh herbs on the windowsill.

Edgewater. She had to work on the Edgewater proposal, trying to win business to *prove herself,* when the "win" was probably as sealed and decided as this very "arrangement" that had been orchestrated behind her back.

What a farce. Damn her father. Damn her manipulating, untrustworthy father.

The solution presented itself as clearly as the historic drawings she'd been admiring the night before. Daddy was in for a rude awakening when it came time for the final Edgewater presentations. A very rude awakening. She couldn't—she *wouldn't*—be manipulated.

"Actually, Colin and I will be working together from now on."

This time, he did look surprised, looking over his shoulder with a wide-eyed expression. "Is that so?"

"Yes, it is. In fact—" she turned to the cabinet to get another cup "—I think I'll take him some coffee so we can get started nice and early."

"Oh, of course." The unflappable Lenny sounded a little…flapped. "Would you like me to serve breakfast in the studio?"

"No, thank you," she said, pouring some coffee and scooping up the mug with her free hand. She walked out of the room, adding, "We'll want complete privacy. We'll come downstairs when we've…had enough."

A week later, they still hadn't had enough. At least, it felt that way to Grace. Seven days after her change of allegiance from Edgewater to Pineapple House, the only thing that marred the intimate, newfound joy of Grace's days—and nights—was the secret that she kept from her lover.

She sat on the studio floor, her legs folded under her denim skirt, her fingers tapping to the light jazz music they'd finally agreed on. All around her were the new sketches of Pineapple House they'd been jointly creating nearly every minute that they weren't…doing other things.

Lots of other *wonderful* things.

Like taking showers together, one of Colin's favorite activities, especially when it involved a great deal of soap and shampoo and time. Or strolling along Cliff Walk at midnight, sharing kisses and conversation before they headed back for another night of seemingly endless love-making punctuated by bad puns, long cuddles and possibly another shower. And eating. Oh! Could the man eat. Gourmet dinners on the patio and picnics on the lawn and breakfast in bed.

If Leonard was aware that their relationship had turned intimate over the previous week, he was too much of a professional to show it. Of course, she'd kept all her clothes and personal belongings in her room, making her turned-back bed every morning after she'd spent the night with Colin. For all the butler knew, they had simply buried their differences and were sharing ideas. At least, Grace hoped that was what he communicated to her father every morning.

The thought of it made her chest constrict with concern. What would happen when Colin found out? Of course, this was a temporary relationship. He lived in Pittsburgh and had made his lack of interest or belief in love pretty clear. His disdain revealed itself in the form of a dozen different subtle comments, ranging from mocking his brother's recent engagement to several references to himself as a confirmed bachelor. No. She knew what this was and she accepted that.

This was purely physical. An affair. An interlude. A magical time with the most sensual man she'd ever met. But she remained certain that he would be livid if he knew they were both being manipulated in Eugene Harrington's schemes. The thought of it sickened her.

"Well, what do you know about that?"

She looked up at where he sat, perched on a stool between the CAD workstation and the high drafting table. "About what?"

He held up a finger and turned to a massive file that they'd gotten from the archives of the zoning office they'd visited the day before. "Just a sec, I want to check something."

She watched him peruse the file, click a few keys on the computer, and go back to the file. She took a minute to drink in the gorgeous image he made, loving the little wireless reading glasses he wore perched on his nose when he worked on the CAD system. His hair was down, at *her* request, his morning stubble unshaven. He'd shave later, she knew. Before they went to bed.

"Oh, man," he said softly.

She pushed herself off the hardwood floor and walked over to him, absently rubbing his shoulders as she peered into the computer. "What is it?"

He turned around, taking the glasses off and sliding his hands around her waist. "I love when you rub my back."

With him on the stool, they were eye to eye. Face-to-face. Mouth to mouth. "I love when you rub my front," she teased, tangling his hair around her fingers and breathing in the delicious, familiar scent of him. "What did you find?"

He shook his head, looking a little torn between the sexual play they were forever engaged in and whatever had caught his attention in the file. "Just a little glitch in the zoning law. Someone could actually make the argument, according to what I just read, that the lot where Pineapple House stood is a separate parcel from Edgewater."

"Really? How can that be?"

"Some ancient residential districting loophole, if I'm reading my New England real estate language correctly."

She looked over his shoulders to the Web page on his computer. "What does it mean?"

He shrugged. "I'm not sure. I may run it by my brothers. Cameron's an investment banker and lawyer who knows New York and Connecticut law. Rhode Island probably isn't that different. And Quinn understands every nuance of real estate known to man." He pulled her into his chest and tucked her between his legs, his hands wandering possessively under the tank top that she wore. With no bra. At *his* request. "Now what was that about your front?"

As always, she melted against him. The man had an absurd amount of power over her body. She refused to stop and think about it. Just as she refused to think about…the secret. Was there any way she could avoid telling him? Maybe. Maybe if they had a killer presentation that she could take to her father and demand that H&H offer it to Adrian. Colin would be satisfied with that; he had not insisted on ownership of the concept or the bid. He just wanted Pineapple House to be built.

If she told him what she knew about her father and Adrian Gilmore, everything might come to a crashing, untimely end. And she just wasn't ready for that. Not yet.

His hands stilled against her ribs. "What are you thinking about, Gracie?"

She struggled to find a quick answer. She'd gotten very good at avoiding anything that resembled a substantial conversation, which was so easy to do when they both let their bodies do the talking. But Colin was honest, and he expected the same from her.

The weight of worry pressed harder on her chest. She was not being honest. So far from it.

"I'm just tired," she said vaguely. "Maybe we should take a break."

"Great idea," he agreed with a kiss on her nose. "How about a trip to Willow House?"

She brightened immediately. "I'd love to see Marguerite again. Why don't we see if we can pilfer something from Lenny's fridge and take her something special?"

The thought of the butler deepened the hole in her heart. How long could she wait to tell Colin the truth?

He turned to click the Off switch on the computer. "She'd like that." He surprised her by spinning back around on the stool and taking her face in his hands, giving her a deep, sexy kiss. "Remind me to spoil you rotten in bed tonight."

How long could she wait?

As long as possible.

Colin tapped on the door of Willow House room number seven as the sound of Gracie's delightful laugh echoed down the hushed hallway. He loved that he could make her laugh so easily, even with a string of horrendous architectural puns that had become their favorite word game.

"Now that's a beautiful sound to these old ears." Marguerite's delicate voice greeted them as Colin nudged the door with his shoulder and held it open for Gracie.

He set the soft-sided cooler that Leonard had packed on the floor and made his way around the bed. Marguerite had told him when she'd moved into the house that she liked it when he sat with the window behind him because she could make out his silhouette. He'd made a point of going there as soon as he got to her room.

Perching on the side of the bed, he scooped up her withered old hands and reached over to kiss her wisps of white hair, taking a quick whiff of the light fragrance of talcum powder. "How's my best girl doing today?"

Her wrinkles deepened with a knowing smile. "I think I've been replaced." With an effort, she turned to the other side of the bed, where Gracie had taken a seat in the single guest chair. "I could hear you lovebirds laughing in the hall."

He saw Gracie flush in the dim light, but an odd sense of pride filled him. How could he not be proud that anyone would imagine Gracie in love with him? As if.

"No one can replace you," Gracie assured her, her voice somehow a mixture of cool elegance and personal warmth. She had a gift for making people feel comfortable—a waiter, the butler, even sweet old Vera out front was charmed by her.

"Colin talks about you all the time," she said to Marguerite, pulling the chair closer so his grandmother could see her. Or feel her, as she often did. "He's told me all the wild stories about the Rebels."

Marguerite managed a sly look at him, then turned back to Gracie. "All true, I assure you. I have a colorful and checkered past. I hope St. Peter is in a forgetful mood when I get up there."

Gracie patted her hand. "I understand he takes in all aspects of the situation," she said with a smile. "You're forgiven certain misdeeds if they were done for the right reasons."

Marguerite sighed. "I hope you're right, my dear. I think I'm soon to find out."

"No," Colin insisted, a familiar ache taking up too much space in his chest. He hated the thought of losing her. Hated the inevitable pain. Sure she was old. But she was...special. "You have a few important dates on your calendar, Marguerite, and none involve St. Peter. We need you as Mistress of Ceremonies for the Pineapple House groundbreaking, of course, and you have to dance with me at the Grand Opening party."

Even as he made the promises, he knew they were empty. She'd never make the groundbreaking.

"Gracie can have all my dances," she said, smiling benevolently at him. "But I'll be there in spirit, darling boy." As though to underscore that thought, she coughed and Gracie started to get up to get her water. "No, no," Marguerite insisted, patting Gracie's hand again. "I'm fine. I want to hear about Pineapple House. Tell me what you two are doing to make my dream come true."

He and Gracie shared a look, and she gave him a nod of silent permission. He half smiled in return, the dull pain in his chest easing immediately. God, he adored her.

"Gracie's had some amazing ideas, Marguerite," he began. "Wait until you see what she came up with to recreate the old stairway. There's a technology now…"

He paused as Marguerite held up a hand as though to quiet him, but she merely wanted to touch Gracie's face. It was her only way of really seeing someone and Colin was grateful that Gracie understood and let her. Someone else might be put off by the intimate gesture, but Gracie leaned forward and let Marguerite examine her as though it were the most natural thing in the world.

"Go on," said Marguerite, as she laid her palm on Gracie's cheek and began her tactile exploration. "I want to hear about the stairs. But I also want a good look at the woman you love."

He opened his mouth to speak, but no words came out.

The woman he loved.

Unable to stop himself, he looked over his tiny grandmother at Gracie, but she'd closed her eyes. And smiled. Marguerite stroked a finger over a single spot on Gracie's cheek. Was that why she was smiling? Or was it in response to the words that hung in the air?

"Oh!" the older woman exclaimed with a tiny burst of surprise. "You have dimples."

This time Gracie looked up and winked at him.

"Yeah," Colin agreed, meeting her gaze. "She's basically the prettiest girl you've ever seen, Marguerite."

"Oh, that's obvious," Marguerite replied.

Gracie's smile turned self-conscious, and she shook her

head as though they were both out of their minds. "Are you hungry, Marguerite?" she asked. "We have a little treat for you."

His grandmother nodded and her eyes lit up like a little child's. "Yes, please! They gave me something dreadful and green for lunch. I'd simply cry for chocolate. My sweet tooth is screaming at me."

Gracie chuckled. "We have just the cure for that." She went to the cooler and waved a hand at Colin. "Tell her about the staircase while I get the chocolate mousse."

"Chocolate mousse?" Marguerite's voice went up half an octave with delight. "Oh, this is my lucky day."

As Colin explained Gracie's idea—and it *was* brilliant—for reproducing the one-of-a-kind colonial staircase in Pineapple House, Gracie helped Marguerite quiet her sweet tooth.

He tried to concentrate on describing the stair design, but watching this classy, beautiful woman spoon-feed high-end pudding to Marguerite blew his concentration. In fact, the sight of them together did the stupidest things to his insides. His heart, in particular, felt heavy and full. And his throat kept closing up.

Where did he ever get the impression that Grace Harrington was a cold, stuck-up rich girl who looked down at him? She was nothing of the sort. She had a heart of pure gold and a soul as gentle as spring wind. She was kind, patient, funny, sensual, bright, unselfish and real. She was…*the woman he loved.*

"She's asleep," Gracie whispered, pulling him out of his reverie. She carefully dabbed the older woman's lips. "We've tired her out with the technology of staircases, I'm afraid."

He looked at her, his heart damn near ready to explode the way his body did when he was inside her. What was going on? What were these words that were ridiculously close to spilling from his lips?

This was insane. He'd fallen in love. Only one thing could happen now. She'd betray him. *Wouldn't she?*

He knew that. Hadn't that been the one lesson his mother had taught him as a child? Love meant betrayal, pain and loss. And a lifetime of *hurt*.

"What's the matter, Colin?" She reached over and touched his hand. "Are you all right?"

"I'm just—" He shook his head and said the only thing he ever could when asked a question. The truth. "I'm scared."

She squeezed his hand, a definite dampness filling her eyes. "I know. But she's lived a long life and you've done so much to make her even happier. And she just might see that groundbreaking party. You never know."

"Yeah, you're right," he said, snapping out the light so Marguerite could rest. With an effort, he swallowed the words that threatened to wreck his carefully protected shell. He managed three different words. "You never know."

Ten

It seemed as if Colin couldn't drive any faster to get them home. He zipped his little sports car around the turns of Newport and accelerated through every intersection. His hand rested firmly on Grace's leg, moving only to shift gears and immediately returning to a solid grip.

Since they'd left Willow House, he'd been distant and distracted, his eyes as stormy as whatever emotional disturbance was brewing inside him.

Scared, he'd said. Obviously, he loved his grandmother, loved the connection to a side of the family he'd never known. He'd admitted that much during one of their long conversations. But it really didn't make sense to be *scared.* Marguerite was well into her nineties. She wasn't in pain or misery. Oddly enough, the older woman seemed to accept the end of her time on earth more easily than Colin did.

Was he scared he might not complete her dream, might not have the opportunity to see Pineapple House built?

The thought reminded her once again of the sickening secret she was keeping from him. There was no way she could let this go on. He had to know. Then they could be even more determined—together—to ensure that even if her father somehow fixed the bidding, H&H would go in with Pineapple House. But even as she harbored that fantasy, she knew the truth.

He was going to be furious. Especially now that she'd let a week pass. She had to tell him. *Now.*

She glanced at him, noting the set of his jaw, the slight frown that creased his forehead. So she remained silent, letting the wind whip around the convertible, filling the air between them with the salty, September tang of the sea. There was no sun, just thick, gray cloud cover that left the chill of impending rain.

She felt, rather than heard him sigh as he pulled into the driveway of Edgewater's carriage house and parked the car next to her Audi.

"Back to work?" she asked tentatively, imagining a quiet hour in the studio to break the news.

He turned to her, his expression serious and unwavering as his gaze dropped over her face. He regarded her with the same intensity she'd seen when they made love, when all defenses were down and he lost himself in a moment of sexual satisfaction.

"I'm going to take a walk." His voice rasped with the announcement.

She had to tell him. *Now.* Regardless of his pensive mood. "I'll come with you."

He glanced at her, a light of surprise in his eyes, then he looked up at the sky. She'd just seen the shadows of precipitation in the rain-laden clouds. They'd get soaked if they walked for more than ten minutes. "All right," he said simply.

She silently thanked him for not insisting she change from

her denim skirt and flat shoes, because she was certain if she'd gone into the house, he'd be gone when she returned. She wiggled her toes, confident that she could navigate the rocks and ledges in loafers and tugged at the hem of her fitted skirt. She'd be fine. She'd risk a little discomfort not to lose this opportunity.

After he'd closed up the car, they joined hands and took the familiar route to the gated entrance to Cliff Walk. Grace untied the cotton sweater she had knotted around her shoulders and pulled it over her head, grateful for some protection against the ocean breeze. Autumn was descending in a big hurry over Newport, sending the temperatures below seventy on a cloudy day.

"It seems like winter's coming faster this year," she said, only to make conversation, as they navigated the first smooth ledge of the Walk.

"Yeah."

He didn't want to talk, she could tell. So she clamped her lips together and decided to wait until the right moment. His mood still seemed somber, anyway. And she sure wasn't about to improve it.

They made their way over some jagged rocks, descending a few broken steps to the regular path, which was deserted on this weekday afternoon in the fall. They had passed one other couple deep in conversation, but Grace couldn't see anyone else for the whole section of Cliff Walk ahead of them. She glanced at the threatening sky again, but resisted the urge to comment on it.

The wind picked up, slicing her bare legs with a sudden whipping chill. She concentrated on her feet, determined not to trip on the irregular rocks.

They walked for fifteen minutes to Rough Point Bridge, where the locals were known to say the real Cliff Walk adventure began. Grace had been there before, but the view of waves crashing below into swirling blue-black water never failed to impress her. They paused for just a second on the rickety metal, just long enough for a few fat drops of rain to hit them.

"Here it comes," she said, holding out a palm to the sky. "We'd better get to one of the tunnels."

There were at least three passages dug into the rocky cliffs within a five-minute walk, all built as access for residents from the various mansions and homes along Cliff Walk.

"Gull Rock is the closest," Colin said, raising his face to the silvery sky as several drops hit his cheeks, forming rivulets over the dark stubble. "We can go there until it clears."

Yet he made no effort to leave the bridge, even as the velocity of the drops hitting them increased.

"Are you going to tell me what's on your mind?" she finally asked.

Saying nothing, he remained perfectly still, the rain running down his cheeks like tears, an image that moved her heart as a priceless work of art would.

His opened his eyes and looked down at her. "Yes."

Before she could respond, he took her hand and started off the bridge, breaking into a fast walk, since running on the rocks was out of the question.

"Come on," he urged. "Let's get to the tunnel."

Wordlessly, they trekked as the rain increased to a steady downpour, soaking through her sweater, plastering the white tank top she wore underneath against her skin. She couldn't move as quickly as he could, and it took nearly ten minutes to reach the portal of Gull Rock Tunnel.

They dashed into the opening, skidding along the dirt into the middle of the tunnel, which was no more than twenty feet long. Inside it was nearly black, the openings at either end providing just enough light for them to find their footing.

Grace squeezed the water out of her hair and wiped her face

with her fingers, watching Colin give his mane a solid shake that sprayed water on the walls. It seemed he was trying harder to shake something out of his head than to sluice water off his long hair.

She leaned against the cool surface of the wall, the echo of their labored breathing bouncing around the tiny space. Suddenly, Colin turned to her, slapping his hands hard against the tunnel, on either side of her head. He looked down at her, that black turbulence still darkening his eyes, his wet hair and gold earring giving him a menacing, piratelike look.

Grace looked up at him, not knowing whether to expect a kiss, a curse, or an explanation.

"I am completely unprepared for this," he said, his voice tight with emotion. "I don't think I'm even capable of…this."

She frowned, looking hard at his expression, trying to figure out what he was saying and to prevent her heart from dropping any farther into her stomach. "Of what?"

"Of loving you."

The words reverberated through the tunnel.

Grace stared at him. "Of…" She couldn't repeat them. She waited for him to say it again.

"I want you to understand something." He dipped his face lower, near enough to kiss her, but he just consumed her with one long, black, hungry gaze. Her eyes adjusted to the dim light, the heat of his body practically creating steam against her soaked clothes and hair. "I'm not the man for you."

She resisted the sudden urge to seize him by the collar, shake him and kiss him, tell him how *wrong* he was, but managed to find a shaky voice. "I think I am the person to decide that."

"No," he insisted, giving his head one violent shake. "You can't—you don't know what—"

She couldn't stop herself. Her fingers curled around the wet fabric of his shirt and she yanked him into her. "Why would you sabotage this, Colin? Can't you even give us a chance?"

He closed his eyes and let out a long, slow breath. When he finally looked at her, the storm in his eyes had subsided just as the one outside became more insistent.

"Gracie, I don't *believe* in the kind of love you have dreams of finding. You know how some people don't believe in God, or they don't believe in—in…" He shook his head in frustration. "They don't believe in anything abstract or esoteric?"

She just stared at him, refusing to say yes. Refusing to help him take this path. *Don't do this, Colin.* She bit her lip and listened, willing her heart not to break.

"Well, I don't believe in that concept of love. I think people can only love themselves. At least, eventually. Once the bloom, or whatever, wears off, people really only care about themselves and someone always gets hurt."

Did he really believe that? Was that his mother's legacy—a lesson that you can never be loved? Surely someone in his life had shown him differently. "What about your grandmother?"

He frowned at her. "Marguerite? What about her?"

"No." Gracie relaxed her grip on his shirt, but didn't let go completely. "The one who raised you. She gave up her life, moved in with you, raised you and your brothers. She loves you."

"Yeah, but—"

"And what about your brothers? They love you. And your father. He—"

He cut her off by banging one of his hands against the tunnel wall. "No, you're talking about family. That's different. That's unconditional and those people don't have a choice."

A choice. Did she have a choice about this? Without a doubt, she did not. "When you love someone, Colin, do you think you have a choice?"

And as she said the words, the revelation washed over her, soaking her as thoroughly as the rain had. Did she really have a choice? Even if he didn't believe in love and left her the minute their imposed time together ended, wouldn't she still feel this heart-ripping emotion every time she saw his face, heard his name, thought of him? Wouldn't she rather be with Colin McGrath than with anyone else, anywhere else, in the world?

Yes, of course. She was already in love. The choice had been made for her.

The knowledge left her reeling, dizzy. She wanted to love him. Needed to love him. But what was he saying? That he wasn't capable of it?

"You always have a choice," he argued, his voice rough, but his hands tender as he grasped her shoulders. "And I strongly suggest you make the right one."

All that mattered, all that was real in that one suspended moment of time settled in a warm cloud around Grace's heart. She had given her virginity to the man she loved. She *had*.

"I already made a choice," she whispered, the rain thundering against the rock overhead so loudly that she could barely hear herself speak. She gathered his shirt again and pulled him closer to her face. "I chose you."

The certainty and rightness of it sang through her like lightning in her veins.

She loved Colin McGrath. Loved his heart and his soul and his brain and his body. She would do anything for him, anything to be with him, anything to make his life better.

Then she remembered the *secret* she'd yet to share. She had to tell him what she'd learned about her father. She couldn't profess love, with something as ugly and unspoken hanging between them. She had to tell him both truths—the good and the bad.

"I want to tell you something," she said softly.

He put his hand over her lips. "Don't say it."

She shook her head. "I have to."

"No," he insisted, removing his hand and replacing it with his mouth, kissing her lightly, then intensifying the connection into a long, delicious affair. "Ah, honey," he sighed into her mouth, exchanging breaths. "I don't know what the hell I've gotten myself into, but I'm in so deep I can't see the light. You are perfect, Gracie. You've always been so perfect, and I'm…I'm not."

Perfect? He might change that opinion as soon as he heard about her father's backstage puppeteering. She put her hand over his wet shirt, widening her palm against his chest to feel the slow, steady drumming of his heart. She took a deep breath of musky, damp air mixed with rainwater and that singular scent of Colin.

How could she say this?

"I have to tell you something," she said.

"No, no." He silenced her with a kiss that burned the words back into her throat, where they stayed to strangle her. Instead, their tongues came together in a heated, hungry exchange, punctuated by Colin pressing his whole, hard, male body against Grace. "I'm first on this one."

On *what* one?

"Listen to me, Colin."

"Listen to *me,*" he countered by rocking against her stomach. The familiar weakness in her legs threatened as the fire started to burn at her core. The flames licked between her pelvic bones as he pressed and moved, moaning softly as he gently lifted her to her tiptoes to increase the coverage of their bodies.

"Colin—"

"Shh." He quieted her with another kiss, his tongue teasing her mouth open, then exploring her teeth, her lips. "Not yet, honey. Wait."

He slid his hand under her sweater and peeled the tank top away like a second skin he had to get under. He hungrily explored her dampened flesh with both hands, covering her breasts and torturing her nipples into aching, bursting buds. Fire and heat seared through her, and for one timeless moment, she forgot everything but the maddening pleasure of his hands and his body grinding against her.

"Here, Gracie. Now. Make *love* to me." The emphasis in his gravelly voice was unmistakable.

Love. Beautiful, dangerous, elusive love.

Burying her face in his neck, she sucked on his wildly beating pulse, tasting salt and rain and sweat as he reached down and pulled her skirt up, bunching the denim at her waist. The sudden rush of air on her exposed body made her shiver, just as he slid his hand down the front of her panties. With a murmur of ecstasy reverberating from his chest, he curled his fingers into the wetness between her legs.

Words were lost in the rush of arousal and need, and Grace snuffed out the thought that once again they were talking with their bodies. He wanted to say something and, damn, she wanted to hear it. Even if it was body to body.

"Make love to me."

He said it again as he pushed her panties down to her knees, and she shimmied out of them completely. Their mouths merged in another heated kiss as he unfastened his pants and freed himself in one quick movement. Grace moved her hand automatically to stroke him, unable to stop herself, unwilling to think about where they were, exposed to the elements and the possibility of discovery.

Nothing mattered but this need. This moment. This *man* she loved.

Scooping her bottom with two strong hands, he lifted her off the ground, until his throbbing, stiff erection slid right between her legs. There was no condom; there were no sheets, no bed, nothing to make this traditional. She shook with the fury of her own excitement, not caring about anything but having Colin inside her.

He said her name and swore softly as she wrapped her legs around his hips and lowered herself onto him. A rush of pain and pleasure collided as they came together, making her buck against him. She tensed her leg muscles to raise and lower herself over his erection, watching the rain mix with sweat to create a sheen on his face. He squeezed his eyes closed and thrust furiously into her.

The familiar twist coiled inside her as she ignored all the discomfort of the wall and let the thrill ride start. She clamped her legs around him as he plunged deeper and harder and faster, his powerful arms holding her up and carrying her over a now-familiar precipice.

Only this was anything but familiar. This exchange was fueled by emotion and the impossible promise of love. She could read it in his eyes, feel it in the passion of every stroke, taste it in each desperate kiss.

She tightened around him, the fury and friction building to one white-hot spot inside her.

"Come with me," he urged, burying himself so far in her she could feel him touch her womb. "Come with me, Gracie. Now."

With three vicious pumps, he expanded, filling her, burning her flesh as he halted and then exploded into her with one, long, soulful groan of wild, uninhibited pleasure. The sound, the sight, the intensity of his orgasm pushed her over the edge, and, helpless, she fell into the same sweet, spiraling ride.

Her head dropped against his chest, her legs trembling and quaking around his waist. Barely able to breathe or think about what they'd just done, she finally looked up to meet his gaze, prepared for his smile, prepared for him to ease her to the ground, but utterly unprepared for what she saw.

That wasn't sweat. That wasn't rain. Not this time.

"I love you, Gracie."

His voice cracked and she started to cry, too.

Colin eased himself out of Gracie, satisfied and spent, but taken aback by the tears that filled her green eyes.

"What's the matter, honey?"

She just shook her head and stared at him. "You're crying."

He put his hand to his face, stunned. "I am?" With a little laugh, he wiped his cheek and looked at his fingertips as though they were covered in contaminated waste. "Jeez. You're good."

Oh, man. He was totally unglued.

She still clung to his neck, their exposed flesh glued together from sweat and rain and sex. The only sound in the cave was their breathing. The rain had stopped.

All he wanted to do was tumble to the ground and hold her and tell her he loved her a thousand more times. The admission of love felt as good as…the act of love.

Instead, he gently eased her down to the ground, then adjusted himself and zipped up his jeans. Still holding her gaze, he bent down to retrieve her underpants.

They hadn't used a condom. A sickening sensation grabbed his gut. But that was the least of his problems. She'd yet to respond to his confession. Did she love him?

Maybe she thought it was a moment-of-passion thing. "I meant it," he said, watching every nuance of her expression for some form of communication.

But she looked away, studying her feet as she eased her skirt back over her hips and thighs. Well, now. That wasn't exactly the *I love you, too,* he'd been hoping for. Wasn't this the girl who was looking for lifelong love from her sex partner?

"I—I'm glad," she said weakly.

He clenched his solar plexus as though it had been punched, but managed a half smile. "That's funny. You don't look glad."

"Well…I…" She almost lost her balance trying to pull her underwear on and he grabbed both arms to steady her. She laughed self-consciously. "They come off easier than they go on."

This was great. She was making jokes. Avoiding eye contact. Changing the subject. He didn't say anything as she righted herself and finished dressing.

"Colin. I have to tell you something."

Yeah, you do. Pulling her closer, he tipped her chin towards his face with one hand, his heart up to a full-blown hammer now. "What is it?"

"I have some…news."

He leaned back to look at her, seeing the trepidation in her expression. "Why do I think I'm not going to like this?"

"'Cause you're not," she said flatly.

She didn't love him. "Hit me, honey."

"My father and Adrian Gilmore organized this…this three-week trial…over a month ago."

For a second, he reveled in relief. She hadn't said "I don't love you." But…what had she said? "What do you mean? I don't get it."

"Neither do I," she said. "But for some reason, my father and Gilmore arranged this…this showdown between us."

"How do you know?"

"I overheard Leonard talking to my dad about a week ago and I realized that this whole thing was prearranged—"

"A week ago?" His voice echoed in the chamber of the tunnel. "You've known this for a *week?*"

A week. The entire time they'd been…sleeping together.

She nodded, worrying her bottom lip with her front teeth. "I didn't know how to tell you."

He took a step back, breaking their contact. "How about, 'Oh, Colin, you'll never believe what I just found out?' That would have worked."

He heard the sarcasm in his voice, but pushed aside any inclination to remove it. How could she do this? How could she know something like that and not share it with him?

She'd lied. Concealing the truth was the moral equivalent of a lie in his book.

"Have you confronted your father?"

She shook her head. "No. I wanted Leonard to report back that we were working together—"

"What?"

She startled at the bellow of his voice. "Not—not for—"

"You mean you're just working on this project with me as a sham—a deception for your father?" *More* lies.

"No!" She put her hands on his chest, but he backed away. "Absolutely not, Colin. I want to present the ideas to him and see if he'll go for it. You told me you didn't care if Hazelwood and Harrington got the business, as long as Pineapple House is built. It was *your* idea that I present it to Gilmore."

He just shook his head, still unable to comprehend what she was telling him. It was fixed. The whole deal was fixed. Eugene Harrington had made a total fool out of him. There was no chance that McGrath, Inc., would get the work. This was a setup.

"Why would they put you…or me through this? What's the point?" He posed the question more to himself than Gracie.

"I have no idea," she assured him. "I really don't. But I won't let him win at this game, Colin. I'm going in with Pineapple House. Honestly. I promise."

He took a few steps away from her, toward the opening of the tunnel and much-needed air. Why had Harrington done this? And, why, good God, why hadn't Gracie told him?

She was right, he thought as he dug the toe of his hiking boot into the muddy opening. It didn't matter who got the business, as long as Pineapple House was the result.

But, damn it, it mattered now. Because he'd been used. And without a doubt, H&H had sewn up this deal a long time before Gilmore went through the charade of presentations.

And wasn't that the way things ran in this world? The rich in control, the powerful pulling strings. The very injustice that Marguerite had been fighting her whole life.

He felt her tentative grasp on his elbow and he resisted the urge to shake her off. Instead, he turned, this time unmoved by the streaks of tears on her cheeks.

"Why didn't you tell me?" he demanded.

"Because I didn't want this…this thing between us to end."

This *thing* between them. It was a *thing* to her.

"And because what we're doing with Pineapple House— it's brilliant. I'm so proud of it."

The sound of his *I love you* echoed in his head as if he'd just screamed it out in the tunnel. What a jerk. What a stupid, lovesick jerk.

No wonder she hadn't said she loved him. She was as much a user as her father. She'd go waltzing into H&H with killer ideas and emerge the darling of the firm. And have a little good *thing* on the side from the chump they'd brought in as a shill.

Puzzle pieces snapped into place in his head with the sound of each crashing wave far below the cliffs. "When, exactly, did you learn this, Gracie?"

She looked at the ground, then up at him. "The morning after…we…when I went downstairs to get coffee."

He felt his jaw go slack. "The very first day?"

She nodded.

"Great. That's just great, Gracie."

"Colin, listen to me. My father's done this to me his whole life." Her eyes filled with tears again. "He's always manipulating me. This time, I wasn't going to let him win."

He let out a disgusted laugh. "Oh, yeah. So you jumped right on the deception bandwagon and took me along for the ride."

"No!" Her voice tightened with frustration. "It wasn't anything like that."

Turning away from her, he leaned against the edge of the tunnel opening and stared out at the silver caps of froth churning on the Atlantic Ocean.

If he backed away now, just on foolish principle, Pineapple House would probably never get built. If he didn't back away, it was a moot point, because Eugene Harrington had won the bid and would put whatever the hell he wanted on the property.

What a crock. H&H had won the bid. That was a given.

So he'd have to fight this a different way. He'd have to fight it the way Marguerite and the Restoration Rebels would. With brains and creativity.

He turned to Gracie and suddenly the losses mounted as quickly as the ironies. When they'd arrived here, she'd wanted love, he'd wanted sex. Now, she'd got all the sex she could possibly handle, and he'd gone and fallen in love.

Pineapple House was the least of his problems. He *loved* her. And she'd betrayed him.

Good to know some things were still predictable.

"I'm leaving. I'll call Gilmore and tell him I'm out."

He heard her little intake of breath. "How can you do that? How can you give up your dreams?"

"I'm not giving up anything." He started out to the path, without waiting for her.

"What about Pineapple House, Colin?" Her voice faded as he walked into the wind, but he heard her add, "What about us?"

He turned and looked at her. "Us?" The cold Atlantic air stung his eyes. At least, he hoped it was the air. "There's no *us*. It was just a game and you…broke the rules." He let out a rueful laugh that got caught in the wind. "Who knew you'd turn into such a master rule-breaker, Gracie?"

He continued down the path, stabbing his hands deep into his jeans pockets and shaking a strand of hair out of his face. After a few minutes, he spun around to see where she was.

Gone. She'd disappeared out the other side of the tunnel and was probably halfway across the grass of the adjacent property. She'd be back on Bellevue Avenue before he was.

Every instinct told him to go after her. Yeah, and every instinct had told him to bare his soul about twenty minutes ago.

Forget that. This time, he ignored his instincts, swallowed the unfamiliar lump in his throat, and he walked back alone, mentally outlining a bleak future that would never include...*the woman he loved.*

Eleven

"**M**r. Harrington's on the line with London, Grace, and he does not want to be disturbed."

Grace clenched her jaw and looked hard at Evelyn Ginsberg, her father's secretary for as long as she could remember. They'd always shared a friendly, if distant, relationship.

"I'm going in there," Grace announced, pausing long enough to give Evelyn a withering look. "He can't put me off for one more minute."

Evelyn pointed to the guest chair next to her desk. "Wait here. I'll see what I can do."

When Evelyn disappeared behind the massive mahogany door to her father's office, Grace dropped into the chair. For two days, she'd been calling her father. She'd tried home, cell, office, golf course and e-mail. He'd never returned a single message.

So returning to Boston was her only option.

Not that leaving Newport had been difficult. The house was

horribly quiet and empty, and she'd done nothing but mope from the moment she'd returned from her two-hour hike around the streets of the city after Colin had walked away from her. Leonard had emerged from the kitchen, looking stricken.

"Mr. Colin has departed," he'd announced quietly.

She hadn't had the heart or energy to question Leonard further. Of course he'd leave. She'd known where this affair was headed from the day she'd crossed the hall and climbed into his bed. He needed an excuse, and she'd handed him one.

I love you, Gracie.

She dug her nail into the leather armrest of the guest chair. No man can be held accountable for what he says at that intimate moment. She'd called Allie and had that confirmed by an expert. They say *anything* at that particular instant, her roommate had proclaimed.

The night he'd left, she'd wandered around the house in a fog as thick as the one that hung over Rhode Island Sound. She curled up in his chair in the studio and cried. She wandered to the veranda and sobbed on the glider under a harvest moon. Unable to sleep in her own bed, she'd finally crossed the hall and climbed into Colin's bed, hugging his pillow and inhaling all that was left of him…his wonderful scent.

Foolish and childish, but comforting.

After two days of trying to concentrate on her assignment instead of her broken heart, she'd packed, said goodbye to Leonard and driven home. She hadn't called Gilmore. She'd let her father handle that. All she wanted to know was…why.

The mahogany door opened enough for Evelyn to slip out, shaking her head. "Not now," she announced softly.

Damn it! Grace shot up from the chair and stormed past the secretary. He would *not* do this. With one quick twist on the knob, she pushed the door open to see the back of her father's head of thick white hair, a cordless telephone pressed to his ear. As always, he stood gazing at the panoramic view of the harbor.

"I want to talk to you," she demanded. "Now."

He spun around at the sound of her voice and glared at her. "Let me call you back. I've got an emergency." His eyes, the same green as her own, locked on her, his black brows raised. Carefully laying the phone down, he indicated a chair with a calm gesture. "Sit down, Grace."

She shook her head, crossing her arms. She wouldn't give him the satisfaction of towering over her while she sat docile in a chair. "I've been calling you for two days."

"I've been very busy," he said vaguely, taking his own chair behind his enormous desk. "Why aren't you in Newport?"

She waited for the familiar grip of nervousness that usually seized her in confrontations with her father, but she remained calm. And for the first time in her life, she actually spoke the words she wanted to, instead of just thinking them. "That's not the right question. The question is why *was* I in Newport?"

"To get the Edgewater business. Business that I have just learned," he glanced at the discarded phone with a disgusted look, "has been reopened for bidding."

"It has?" That didn't make sense. If her father had won the proposal, and arranged the three-week extension, why would Gilmore reopen the bidding?

She took a few steps closer to his desk, glancing at the two pictures beside the phone. One was her, at seven years old on a carousel horse. The other was a formal wedding shot of Eugene and Catherine Harrington. With the way things had been between them for the past fifteen years, it was a wonder he'd kept it there.

"Gilmore just announced a new bid on the property," he said. "He's going to limit it to a few firms, but we're still in."

"I'm surprised. I assumed you had this thing sewn up."

He frowned at her. "Not at all. Everything changed when McGrath dropped out of the original bidding without an explanation. Do you know why?"

"I came here to ask questions, not answer them." The freedom of speaking her mind gave her a little thrill and enough confidence to sit. "I want to know why you arranged that charade and put me in the middle of it."

Her father's eyes narrowed. "Who told you that?"

"I figured it out."

"You're wrong," he insisted.

"You're lying."

"You're wrong about it being a charade."

"Then what the hell would you call it, Dad?"

She didn't know if he flinched at the mild curse, or the sarcastic way she'd said *Dad*.

He cleared his throat. "Well, Grace, in my day, we called it a setup. I don't know what they call it now."

"A setup?" Gracie leaned forward. "What does that mean?"

He pursed his lips and regarded her, then stood to gaze at Boston Harbor. Crossing his arms, he let out a long, gusty sigh. "I was trying to be a matchmaker, Grace."

The blood drained from her head as she processed the word *matchmaker*. "Excuse me?"

"I thought you belonged with him."

She tried to stand, but now her legs refused, so she leaned against the back of the chair and stared at him. Then a short, unbidden laugh burst from her. "You're kidding, right?"

He shook his head. "No, I'm not kidding."

This was a magnitude of manipulation too high even for Eugene Harrington. "You tried to…set me up with Colin McGrath?"

He met her gaze with a defiant stare. "I want you to find love, Grace, is that so hard to understand? I want you to be happier than…" His gaze drifted to the picture by the phone.

"Like every father since the dawn of time, I want something better for you than what I have."

For a long, quiet minute, she just couldn't speak. Finally, she asked, "Don't you trust me to do anything on my own?"

He gave her an unsure smile. "Of course I do. I just thought it was an opportunity to help you along. This young man cares deeply for you."

"How on earth do you know that? You only met him once, right? At a job interview?"

"Yes. And I never forgot him." He cocked his head as though remembering the meeting. "I would have moved mountains to get that architect in H&H, but there was no way he'd ever consider it."

"He's too independent."

He chuckled. "Yes, I suppose that's part of it. But it was you, Grace. He could barely say your name. And when he did, there was a light in his eyes."

Her heart stuttered and then slowed. She'd seen that light. And she'd extinguished it…with the help of her father.

"He told me that he'd always admired you from afar, in college. And he told me that he couldn't work here because of his feelings for you." He swung his desk chair around and sat. "He has integrity, Grace. Talent, integrity and a wealth of feelings for my daughter." He shrugged and nodded in acknowledgement of a mistake. "I thought I'd help things along."

"So you took control and tried to arrange my destiny?"

"I like to control things." He folded his arms and leaned forward. "You inherited that trait."

Fury bubbled up inside her, only to be squashed by common sense and…something else. Oh, yes. Love.

She loved her father. And he, in his clumsy, cold and controlling way, loved her, too. "I just can't believe Gilmore went for it."

"He did, and he agreed to give us his butler to help." He tried to look apologetic. "We understand things didn't end too nicely."

"That would be just how Lenny would understate it."

"Lenny?"

She just shook her head. "Forget it. I have something to tell you."

"Yes?"

"I'm resigning my position. Effective immediately."

His eyes widened as he jumped out of his chair. "What?"

"I'm leaving H&H, Dad. Thank you for the opportunity to be here. I'm going out on my own."

"Grace!" His voiced boomed through the room. "You cannot quit. What on earth will you do?"

"Well," she said as she stood. "The first thing I'm going to do is go after the Edgewater business."

His jaw set in a hard, familiar expression. "If you take our ideas for Edgewater, Grace, it would be a breach of your employment contract." She saw a vein pop in his temple. The one that always danced when he thought he might lose control. "You cannot rebuild Edgewater."

"Don't worry." She gave him a sly smile and pulled her handbag over her shoulder. "I have no intention of rebuilding Edgewater."

He opened his mouth to respond, but she just turned and walked out the door.

The fact that Adrian Gilmore chose Boston as the site for the final round of presentations gave Grace the distinct impression that H&H remained the front-runner for the business. The fact that he'd scheduled the meeting for late on a Friday afternoon meant he expected to entertain the winner of the bid afterward. She smoothed the sleeve of the hot-pink sweater she'd selected for the presentation. She intended to soar today.

She climbed the marble stairs to the second-floor conference rooms at the Ritz Carlton, buoyed by a self-assurance she was still learning to enjoy. It wasn't just the daring sweater and sleek black skirt that gave her the kick of confidence. And she certainly hadn't mended her shattered heart, but starting her own firm and making the final cut for Adrian Gilmore's business had gone a long way to bolstering her sagging ego.

By the end of the day, Harrington Designs would have its first major client. Adrian Gilmore had not confirmed which other firms had made the final selection, but that didn't matter to Grace. Of course she'd be up against H&H, but her ideas would be in a different league from theirs.

Diane, Adrian's secretary, greeted her outside the closed doors. "Hello, Grace. Why am I not surprised that you're first?"

Grace laughed lightly. "Some habits die hard. Can I go in?"

Diane nodded. "Go right ahead. I expect the other two firms shortly and Adrian will be just a few more minutes."

There would be three competitors, then. Thanking Diane, Grace stepped into the empty room, took a seat, and opened her portfolio. The first official presentation of Harrington Designs, Inc., was a good one. She'd every reason to be proud.

She heard her father's laugh as he entered the conference room with Adrian. When they saw Grace, all three exchanged businesslike pleasantries. Adrian had been surprised when Grace had left H&H to start her own firm, but he obviously had enough belief in her work to give her a shot.

He took the head of the table, and her father sat next to him. Looking at his watch, Adrian looked pointedly at Diane in the doorway. "If McGrath isn't here in two minutes, he's out."

McGrath.

Oh, God. Every drop of blood and all that delicious confidence drained away, leaving Grace's arms leaden and a black hole in the vicinity of her stomach. Or was that her heart?

"Don't you dare cut me out, Adrian." Colin's honey-toned voice washed over her at the same time she caught the first whiff of his scent. "I have the winning designs here. And the best team in the world."

Suddenly the room was filled with *men*. Three tall, commanding, overpowering beings all bearing an uncanny resemblance to each other…yet all very different.

One had sandy-blond hair, trimmed flawlessly, and wore an achingly expensive designer suit, custom-cut to fit the expansive man inside it. Next to him, a near carbon copy of Colin, with the same thick dark hair. But his was worn short, except for a wayward lock that fell over his forehead right above striking eyebrows and black-coffee eyes. Dressed in khakis and a navy blazer, no tie, he looked as if he had just stepped off a yacht.

Good heavens. The McGrath brothers had arrived and sucked all the air and life right out of the room.

Behind them, Colin sauntered in, unfazed by his usual late arrival or the fact that he'd tripled the size of his pitch team. Bracing herself for the expected jolt, Grace stood to face him.

At the sight of her, he froze for a fraction of a second, and stared at her, then his gaze flickered over her sweater.

"Hello, Grace."

Grace.

For some reason, that hurt more than anything.

She nodded, keeping her expression as blank as his. "Colin."

A round of hand-shaking broke the awkward moment as Colin greeted Adrian and her father, and introduced his brothers, Cameron and Quinn.

"Sorry about the added population," he said quietly to Adrian. "I really wanted them here because my brothers were instrumental in developing the master plan for Edgewater."

The master plan? Grace's stomach dipped at the thought.

What was he going to present? She'd never counted on competing against Colin. Never dreamed he'd be in this room.

"That's fine," Adrian responded. "We're ready to go. H&H drew number one for presentation, so Eugene will start."

"But…" Colin glanced at Grace, then back at Adrian. "I understood three firms would be competing today."

"There are three firms here." Adrian indicated her father. "Hazelwood and Harrington." He nodded toward Grace. "And the newly formed Harrington Designs."

This time Colin couldn't mask his surprise. "Well. Congratulations, Grace."

Blood banged through her veins, thumping a noisy beat in her ears. She gave him an indifferent smile, totally at odds with the war of emotions raging inside her. "Thank you."

Her father had already begun to set up his slide show, and launched into his opening speech to present the proposed rebuilding of Edgewater.

Grace used every ounce of control to keep her focus on her father, and not give in to the temptation to stare at the men sitting across from her. Even when she felt them sizing her up.

Once, she glanced over and caught Cameron's navy-blue gaze aimed directly at her. His face was more sculpted than Colin's, but no less attractive. He wore a shield of seriousness, this oldest sibling. Suddenly, she found herself wondering how his mother's abandonment had affected him.

Think about *work,* she admonished herself, forcing her focus on her father's presentation. She recognized many of the designs, noting that H&H was recommending a precise replica of the old mansion. On the land where Pineapple House once stood, her father proposed a fountain with a simple pineapple sculpture, a "nod to the past" he said dismissively.

When he had finished, Adrian seemed unmoved. He merely asked Grace to begin.

She had decided not to look at Colin during her whole presentation, certain she'd lose her composure if she did. But when she described what she'd learned about the founders of Newport and the battle for restoration of the original structures, she couldn't resist a glance in his direction.

His expression nearly did her in. She recognized it, having reveled in it so many times during their brief interlude in Newport. His eyes were warm, brimming with affection and admiration.

I love you.

The words reverberated through her head, the way they had in the tunnel that rainy afternoon.

Why had he said that to her? Why had he given her such hope, and then left her without even giving her a chance to explain or talk to her father? She stumbled over a simple phrase and paused to get her thoughts.

Fighting a swell of panic, she coughed, took a drink of water and pressed on, managing to avoid eye contact with Colin for the rest of her presentation for the complete design and rebuilding of Pineapple House on the property where Edgewater had once stood.

When she'd finished, she put her boards in order and quietly walked to her seat. As Colin stood, she caught his gaze.

Leaning over the table, he whispered, "You were fantastic."

Time stood still as a weightless, heart-stopping sensation practically lifted her off the ground. "Thanks," she said with a tight smile, despising the miserable lump in her throat.

And then the three McGraths launched into the task of presenting their proposal and everything simply faded in the background. As Colin spoke, his rich baritone voice filled the room, captivating his small audience.

In faded jeans, a soft-blue shirt, his leather tie-back and earring, he looked more like a renegade rodeo rider than a highly regarded architect. Naturally, he shunned a computer slide show, presenting his ideas as gloriously old-fashioned artist's renderings, each one original and brilliant.

"I propose to divide the grounds of Edgewater into two separate parcels of land," he said, his eyes locked on Adrian as he made his pitch. "The largest parcel will be home to one of the most magnificent mansions ever built in America, a tribute to a bygone Victorian era that celebrated life and success and beauty on a grand scale: the new Edgewater."

The "new" Edgewater featured the mansion's original design, only slightly altered to include a curved roofline and graceful arched windows. The effect was stunning.

"But there will be so much more to Edgewater. First, Quinn will explain the division of the land."

For the next few minutes, Quinn McGrath spoke with the cool authority of someone who understood every nuance of his business, yet managed to infuse his comments with humor and warmth. He explained the loophole in the law that allowed the Edgewater property to be separated, and Adrian listened, rapt.

Colin resumed his pitch and changed the sketch to reveal the familiar elevation of Pineapple House.

"Miss Harrington has done an excellent job of providing the history and importance of this structure. But, instead of a residence, I propose a public building and fully staffed museum that will introduce visitors to the world that existed long before the Gilded Age of Newport. In this scenario, Adrian, you donate this land and building to the City of Newport, to be run by a team of restoration professionals, all descendants of an original group of historians and preservationists."

The Restoration Rebels would live again. A spray of goosebumps blossomed over Grace's skin. What an incredible idea.

At this point, Cameron took over and explained a complicated financing plan that would allow Adrian to fund the entire project, but pay for it from the proceeds of the museum.

"For no financial outlay," Colin added, still looking at

Adrian, "you will be recognized as a hero to all the lovers of history who flock to—and live in—the city of Newport."

The man was a genius. His designs were unparalleled, his plan was daring and yet risk-free, and Adrian Gilmore came away with his mansion *and* a reputation as the savior of the city.

By the time Colin had finished, there was no contest.

Her father's shoulders dropped in nonverbal defeat. Adrian had interrupted Colin twenty times, asking questions, probing for ideas, confirming his delight with the idea.

When the meeting ended, Grace packed her portfolio and planned a quick departure, but a strong hand settled over hers, stopping her. She looked up into deep, unwavering blue eyes.

"I enjoyed your presentation," Cameron said.

"Likewise," she answered. "Colin's plan is brilliant."

He glanced to where Colin stood in conversation with Adrian. "His plan is brilliant, but sometimes my little brother is a bit impulsive. Too honest and stubborn."

She regarded him closely, trying to figure out what he was trying to communicate. "He knows what he wants," she said.

"But he doesn't always trust himself to get it."

She sensed the conversation between Colin and Adrian coming to an end, and, as much as she'd love to stand there and discuss the finer points of Colin McGrath, she had to get away. The tears she'd battled for the past four weeks were threatening to make an unscheduled appearance.

"It was nice meeting you," she said weakly, stuffing the last paper into her portfolio and darting out of the room.

She made it as far as the top of the marble staircase.

"What's the hurry?"

At the sound of Colin's voice, she attempted a bright smile. "I have another meeting." Did he really want to do this? Did he really want to make small talk—or worse, have their goodbye in the lobby of a hotel? "Congratulations, you nailed this one."

Searching her face, he opened his mouth to say something, but Diane came around the corner in a half run.

"Mr. McGrath, please don't leave. Mr. Gilmore would like to speak with you and your brothers."

Colin looked over his shoulder. "In a minute."

Grace nudged him lightly, somehow managing to keep her voice from cracking. "You'd better go. Your *client* wants you."

"You left H&H," he said.

She nodded. "Yep. I'm a free agent."

His jaw tightened, the way it always did when he was fighting the urge to say what he was thinking. "I just—I just had to tell you what a great job you did in there."

"Kind of tough to outshine your crew." She couldn't resist a wink. "That's some gene pool you're swimming in, Colin."

He shrugged. "On my father's side, anyway."

She took one step down the stairs, but paused at the note of pain she heard in his voice. Looking up at him, she reached her hand out to touch his arm. "You're a product of your past, Colin. Good, bad and ugly. What happened to you…well, it made you who you are. And who you are is…" Damn, there went her voice. "…really, really fine." And the tears started.

"Gracie, listen to me—"

"McGrath!" Adrian's voice boomed across the second floor of the Ritz Carlton. "I'm waiting."

He let out a little breath and closed his eyes. "He might be a tough client."

And then it hit her. Why hold back? Why fight for control over something that simply *cannot* be controlled?

She squeezed his arm, and took a deep, courage-building breath. "I love you, Colin. I've loved you for as long as I can remember and I probably always will."

His eyes widened and he started to speak, but suddenly Adrian was marching toward them, eyes blazing. He clamped his hand on Colin's shoulder and pulled him in the opposite direction.

"For God's sake, man, time is money."

She stood at the top of the steps, watching him disappear around the corner. But just before he did, Colin turned back.

"I love you, too." He mouthed the words to her.

Grace stood there for a full five minutes, trying to understand what had just happened.

And then she went home to break her last promise.

She needed a drink.

Twelve

It was nearly eleven when the cab pulled up to the red-brick building that matched the address in the phone book. Colin and his brothers had done their time with Gilmore, which had included a long dinner and a few stops around town. In a noisy Irish pub, Quinn had taken him aside and practically pushed him out the door.

"Listen, we can handle this guy. You get your ass over to wherever she lives and do what you need to do, bro." Quinn's eyes burned with sincerity. "Trust me on this one. Once you find the one for you, you *cannot* let her go."

Colin had answered with an arguably unmanly bear hug, and dashed into the street. The next minute he was shoving money at a surprised Boston cabbie, encouraging him to break a few laws if necessary in order to get to Dartmouth Street in record time.

Colin stood in front of the small apartment building, peering up at the light on the third floor. Luck was with him again—or at least she had been that afternoon when he'd walked into a conference room and seen that amazing woman. And with a little more luck, that light was apartment 3A, Gracie was still awake, and she'd accept the offer he was more than prepared to make. He held the buzzer down and prayed he still had his lifelong good luck.

An unfamiliar female voice answered, and he remembered Gracie had a roommate. Allie. When he told her his name, she hesitated, then buzzed him in. Taking the stairs two at a time, he was just about to knock when the door whipped open.

A beautiful dark-haired girl gave him a dubious once-over, tugging at the ties of her bathrobe.

He glanced down at her slippered feet. "Nice Tweeties," he said with what he hoped was a disarming smile. "Is Gracie here?"

"She's, uh, indisposed, at the moment."

Indisposed? "Can I wait for her?"

She shrugged, holding the door open in invitation. "It could be a while. She was pretty far gone."

"Far gone? Where'd she go?"

The woman crossed the entryway and led him into a living room. She picked up a half-empty bottle of red wine and gave the label a cursory glance. "Somewhere in the Napa Valley."

His jaw dropped. "Gracie? Drank wine?"

"Yep. And it wasn't pretty." She set the bottle down and reached for his hand. "I'm Allison Powers, Grace's roommate."

"Hi, Allie. Gracie's mentioned you. I'm—"

"I know who you are. Mr. King Stud."

"Excuse me?" He laughed at the suggestive way she said it, and remembered a time when Gracie had teased him with the name of a special lumber used for doors. "It's an architect's joke," he explained.

Allie gave him a sly smile. "So I heard. Unfortunately, I was subjected to a whole string of bad building jokes. She's a veritable Frank Lloyd Wright doing stand-up after the first glass of wine."

Oh, no. "The *first* glass?"

He glanced around the living room, recognizing the sexy pink sweater dropped onto the floor, next to a pair of high heels. Oh, man. What happened to Gracie Harrington—virgin, teetotaler and neat freak?

He happened.

"Oh, yeah," Allie added, following his gaze to the floor. "She relieved herself of most of her clothes on glass number two."

Great. Now she was stripping. "Is that when she… crashed?"

Allie blew out an expansive breath as though it pained her to relay the story. "No. The third glass brought the expected onslaught of tears."

His gut tightened. "She cried." So to top it all off, he'd broken her heart.

"Cried? No, that wasn't crying, pal. That was a blubbering waterfall with terminal nose-blowing, full-body shuddering and some really nasty hiccups."

He couldn't stand it anymore, literally having to hold himself back from tearing the little apartment to pieces until he found her and made everything right again. "I need to see her."

Allie looked skeptical. "Well, she's been asleep for several hours. I guess…" She looked over her shoulder to the hallway, then back at him, her dark eyes narrow and accusing. "All I know is that one fairly together woman left here for Newport a month ago, but returned smashed into a million pieces."

"Please," he said softly. "I can fix that."

She regarded him for a minute, and then lifted one pouty lip into a half smile. "She probably won't remember, anyway." She pointed down the hall. "First door on the right. And, whatever you do, go easy on her with that load-bearing beam, buddy."

Smiling, he passed her and headed straight to Gracie.

The room was completely dark, the only sound the familiar rhythm of Gracie's breathing, broken by little quivering sighs on the exhale. His heart nearly folded in half.

In the past four weeks, he'd had a lot of conversations with his brothers and one long heart-to-heart with Marguerite, but none of them could make him see what he'd seen this afternoon in a hotel conference room.

A woman strong enough to hold her own against any level of competition. A woman proud enough to push the envelope and stand up against her manipulative father. A woman with enough control to know when to let go of it.

A woman he loved.

Kicking off his shoes, he slid into the bed next to her. She moaned as the weight of the mattress shifted, rolling over to curl one delicious leg around him. Oh, this was so right. So perfect. How could he ever think he could live without Gracie? Loving her was an honor. A privilege. A fact of his life.

He placed a gentle hand on her shoulder, immediately recognizing the worn cotton fabric of his ten-year-old T-shirt.

He smiled into the darkness and wrapped an arm around her. "Well, what do you know? It's Gracie, sleeping it off in my CMU T-shirt." He kissed her head. "Feels like we've been here before, honey."

She sighed softly, then resumed the steady breaths of sleep.

"But last time, I blew it so bad because I let you go. I shouldn't have done that, Gracie. I should never have let you go ten years ago."

"Mmm. Colin." His name tumbled off her lips as if she'd said it every day.

He stroked her cheek, pushing a few wayward blond strands behind her ear. "I'll never make that mistake again, honey," he promised with another soft kiss on her cheek. "Because for the last four weeks, I've discovered a new law of design. Wanna hear it?"

She remained still.

"The whole world is two-dimensional without Gracie in it. There's no depth. No color. No angles or shapes." He kissed her softly. "I don't like that world, honey. I don't want to live without you."

She inhaled and let out a long slow breath with a whisper of mint. He smiled at that. She hadn't completely changed. Only Gracie Harrington would get plowed on three glasses of wine and remember to brush her teeth before bed.

"I came over to tell you I got the business," he whispered, curling a strand of her hair around his finger. "Adrian called it the best of both worlds. And he told me the whole story about your father and the three-week blind date they sent us on."

Her breathing evened out and for a moment, he thought she might be awake. His eyes began to adjust to the dark and he could see the outline of her beautiful face in repose.

"Imagine that, your father thinking we belonged together."

He heard the hitch in her breathing.

"Funny thing is, we do." He inched her closer into his chest. "And I have a proposal for you." He waited for a reaction to his words, but there was none.

"You did such a great job today. Your ideas were incredible and, man, you were killing me in that sweater."

She flinched just enough for him to suspect she might have heard that. Hoping she had, he continued to whisper quietly in the dark.

"I decided we ought to share this business, Gracie. In fact, I think we ought to make it completely official. Let's rebuild the mansion and create the house and…well, let's just do the whole thing together."

He tunneled his fingers into her hair and tugged her head

into the crook of his neck, so he could breathe his next sentence into her ear.

"Let's merge, honey. One company. McGrath...and McGrath."

He felt her body stiffen. She was awake. His pulse quickened, waiting for her response. "What do you think, Gracie?"

"Either I'm still a little tipsy, or—" she moved her head out of his neck slowly, her eyes clouded with sleep "—I'm having the best dream in the world."

God, she was beautiful. "This isn't a dream and you're sober enough. What do you think of my proposal?"

"Did you say McGrath...and *McGrath?*"

He lifted her chin so he could kiss her lips but before he did, he smiled. "I thought you'd change your name when you marry me, but you don't have to."

He inched forward to kiss her but she backed away. "Are you asking me to marry you, Colin?"

"Honey, I'm not asking, I'm begging." He tightened his embrace and closed his eyes. "I love you, Gracie. I want to spend every day of my life showing you how much I love you."

"Ah, Colin. I love you, too." Her eyes glistened in the dark. "And I'll never hurt you. I'll never betray you or leave you...or stop loving you."

"I know, honey." He swallowed the lump in his throat once and for all. "I know."

She sighed and snuggled back into him. "Please don't ever let me wake up from this dream."

"You better wake up. Because we have stuff to build."

"What kind of stuff?"

"Edgewater. Pineapple House. A business." He paused and held her tighter. "A family. A future. Our life together."

She sighed, resting her head against his chest. His solitary life was over. He'd found the woman he loved.

"When do we start?" she asked.

He slipped his hand under the T-shirt and touched the warm silk of her skin. "Now."

She moaned softly and arched into his body. "On one condition," she whispered, closing her mouth over his earlobe and fluttering the earring with her tongue.

"Anything," he promised as she tugged on the leather strap to free his hair.

She eased her body on top of him, finding that singular place where they melted together. "No rules."

He started to laugh but she quieted him with one long lusty kiss, and then they broke every rule they could remember.

Epilogue

Somewhere in the midst of spring-green leaf buds, a robin chirped its morning song. Grace closed her eyes for a moment, imagining that it was the spirit of Marguerite Deveraux, her tiny voice calling out in appreciation for the gathering that had formed for the groundbreaking of Pineapple House.

They stood in a small circle under the ancient elm tree—Colin and Grace, Quinn and his new bride, Nicole, and Cameron. A cool April breeze wafted over Grace's shoulder, and Colin automatically wrapped an arm around her.

"I guess it's time," he said quietly.

Cameron nodded, bending over to carefully lay the pineapple shaped container into the deep hole that had been dug. It was so fitting that all three McGrath brothers had arrived for the service. The legal and real estate battles they'd waged in the past seven months had been won by an astounding combination of their skills and wit. They clearly had the genes of a Restoration Rebel living in them, and Pineapple House would be built only because of their joint determination to realize their grandmother's dream.

The formal groundbreaking, with the first official shovel of dirt being dug by Adrian Gilmore, would start in about an hour, when the cameras arrived and the Burger Boy billionaire's public relations machine took over.

But this ceremony was a private one. For Marguerite. For family.

Grace's family now. The McGraths. It would be official when they married in a few months, the first ceremony scheduled to take place in Pineapple House. But these men already felt like brothers to her.

As she thought of the tiny woman they'd lost a few weeks earlier, Grace's eyes filled with tears of sadness and joy.

"She was a quiet storm," Colin said, his arm tightening around Grace. "I learned so much from her."

Quinn swallowed and Grace saw his fingers curl around Nicole's hand. "Thanks for finding her, Colin. She was a real gift to us."

Cameron started to say a familiar prayer, and they all softly joined in. As she spoke, something caught Grace's eye, a movement from behind the gate of the Edgewater driveway. No one else seemed to notice, but Grace stole a look, hoping that the locals and media weren't planning to arrive too early for the groundbreaking.

Leaning to her right to see past Quinn, Gracie saw an older woman at the gate, with salt-and-pepper hair and a careworn face. As their gazes locked, another chill rose over Grace's arms. This one not caused by the breeze.

The dark-brown eyes were eerily familiar. They were Marguerite's eyes. Colin's eyes.

Cameron's voice faltered. Grace looked up and saw him staring at the same woman. The color drained from his chiseled features, his eyes flashed midnight blue.

When she looked back to the gate, the woman was gone.

Grace knew who it was. One more member of the family had tiptoed back to Newport to see her three sons lay her mother to rest.

Cameron finished the prayer without any other change in his expression, but she saw him look several times toward the gate.

So their mother had made an appearance but couldn't bring herself to talk to her sons. The thought ripped Grace's heart and she leaned into Colin.

He smiled down at her, his eyes moist at the loss of his beloved Marguerite. Their shared look spoke the words they were both thinking. *I love you.*

Grace dropped her head against Colin's shoulder and made her silent promise to Marguerite. She would spend the rest of her life loving this man, making him whole, healing his wounds and tending to any new ones that life threw their way.

She would always, always be the woman he loved.

* * * * *

Silhouette Desire presents

Annette Broadrick's

second book in her new series

The Crenshaws of Texas

The arousing connection between blue-eyed
Jared Crenshaw and Lindsey Russell was undeniable
from the moment they met. Before he knew it, Jared
had woken up in Lindsey's bed, but how had he gotten
there? He was certain they'd been caught in the
crossfire of somebody's scandalous scheme....

CAUGHT IN THE CROSSFIRE

Silhouette Desire #1610
On sale October 2004

Available at your favorite retail outlet.

From Silhouette Desire
The next romance from

Kristi Gold's
miniseries

THE ROYAL WAGER

When the right woman comes along, all bets are off!

Available October 2004

DARING THE DYNAMIC SHEIKH
Silhouette Desire #1612

Promised to one another at birth, this sheikh
and princess were determined not to be trapped
in a loveless marriage—until they set eyes on one
another after ten long years apart.

If you enjoyed what you just read,
then we've got an offer you can't resist!

Take 2 bestselling love stories FREE!

Plus get a FREE surprise gift!

Clip this page and mail it to Silhouette Reader Service™

IN U.S.A.	**IN CANADA**
3010 Walden Ave.	P.O. Box 609
P.O. Box 1867	Fort Erie, Ontario
Buffalo, N.Y. 14240-1867	L2A 5X3

YES! Please send me 2 free Silhouette Desire® novels and my free surprise gift. After receiving them, if I don't wish to receive anymore, I can return the shipping statement marked cancel. If I don't cancel, I will receive 6 brand-new novels every month, before they're available in stores! In the U.S.A., bill me at the bargain price of $3.80 plus 25¢ shipping and handling per book and applicable sales tax, if any*. In Canada, bill me at the bargain price of $4.47 plus 25¢ shipping and handling per book and applicable taxes**. That's the complete price and a savings of at least 10% off the cover prices—what a great deal! I understand that accepting the 2 free books and gift places me under no obligation ever to buy any books. I can always return a shipment and cancel at any time. Even if I never buy another book from Silhouette, the 2 free books and gift are mine to keep forever.

225 SDN DZ9F
326 SDN DZ9G

Name	(PLEASE PRINT)	
Address	Apt.#	
City	State/Prov.	Zip/Postal Code

Not valid to current Silhouette Desire® subscribers.

Want to try two free books from another series?
Call 1-800-873-8635 or visit www.morefreebooks.com.

* Terms and prices subject to change without notice. Sales tax applicable in N.Y.
** Canadian residents will be charged applicable provincial taxes and GST.
All orders subject to approval. Offer limited to one per household.
® are registered trademarks owned and used by the trademark owner and or its licensee.

DES04R   ©2004 Harlequin Enterprises Limited

COMING NEXT MONTH

#1609 THE LAWS OF PASSION—Linda Conrad
Dynasties: The Danforths
When attorney Marcus Danforth was falsely arrested, FBI agent
Dana Aldrich rushed to prove his innocence. Brought together by the
laws of the court, they discovered their intense mutual attraction ignited
the laws of passion. Yet Dana wanted more from this sizzling-hot lawyer—
she wanted love....

#1610 CAUGHT IN THE CROSSFIRE—Annette Broadrick
The Crenshaws of Texas
The arousing connection between blue-eyed Jared Crenshaw and
Lindsey Russell was undeniable from the moment they met. Before he
knew it, Jake had woken up in Lindsey's bed, but how had he gotten there?
He was certain they'd been caught in the crossfire of somebody's scandalous
scheme....

#1611 LOST IN SENSATION—Maureen Child
Mantalk
Dr. Sam Holden was still reeling from the past when Tricia Wright swept
him up into a whirlwind of passion. This woman was an intriguing force of
nature: blond, bubbly and hot as hell. But their joint future was put
permanently on hold until he could conquer the past that haunted him.

#1612 DARING THE DYNAMIC SHEIKH—Kristi Gold
The Royal Wager
Princess Raina Kahlil had no desire to marry the man she'd been promised
to. That was until she met Sheikh Dharr Ibn Halim face-to-dashingly-
handsome-face. While Raina found herself newly drawn to her culture and
country, she was even more intensely drawn to its future king....

#1613 VERY PRIVATE DUTY—Rochelle Alers
The Blackstones of Virginia
Federal agent Jeremy Blackstone was the only man Tricia Parker had ever
loved. Now, years after they'd parted, she was nursing him back to health.
Tricia struggled not to fall under Jeremy's sensual spell, but how could she
resist playing the part of both nurse *and* lover?

#1614 BUSINESS OR PLEASURE?—Julie Hogan
Daisy Kincaid quit her job when she realized that her boss, Alex Mackenzie,
would never reciprocate her feelings. But when the sexy CEO pleaded for
her to return and granted her a promotion to tempt her back, would the
new, unexpectedly close business-trip quarters finally turn their business
relationship into the pleasure she desired?

SDCNM0904